MY PERSON

G.M. Parrillo

COPYRIGHT

Printed in the United States of America

ISBN 979-8-9928609-5-5

www.gmparrillo.net

Cover Art by: Amanda Kilkenny
Editor: G.M. Parrillo
Guest Editors: Harleen Soare, Jen Xant, Roma Scroggins & Ethan
Morris
G.M. Parrillo Publishing, a subsidiary of The Inkbound Publishing
Roselle Park, NJ

Reviews are the key to an Independent Authors success. Please feel
free to post your review on both Amazon and Goodreads.

Thank you for your consideration.

DEDICATION

To my Fred, thank you for letting me be your Ginger, my bio partner and your friend. I love you to the moon and back, Babycakes!

For those who have never been accepted, who have been shunned, who just need to be allowed to live free without judgment. I will always have all the free mom hugs to give, to walk you down the aisle and march alongside you in the parades.

You are seen, you are loved and you are wanted.

To all my sparkly unicorns, who shine brighter than the sun, my little nuggets of joy – be amazing on purpose!

Love your faces

PROLOGUE

Kevin

October 31, 1995, Tuesday

The stinging cold against his back from being slammed up against the metal locker hurt more than it did the last time this guy had done this, thought Kevin. On Halloween, of all days, how was it that he would be getting bullied by a football player dressed up as cheerleader, but here he was.

As a gay teenage boy; who didn't love a fashion and musical icon like *Cher*? Naturally, on the one day it was socially acceptable to dress up like her, he couldn't resist. But seriously, did Brendan Moser not see the irony in what he was wearing as well? *You couldn't keep your mouth shut could you*, Kevin thought. All he said to Toselle Park's wide receiver was that his wig needed to be straightened. Yet once again, he was getting slammed up against a locker. It seemed to be a once-a-month occurrence with this kid, which made his mind start to wander. An intrusive thought came to his mind. *Maybe Brendan is actually a girl and he is on his period or something.*

As the senior towered over him, Kevin needed to look up due to the age and height difference. The reverberating sound of his own blood pumping in his ears almost deafened him. The taste of warm nickel in his mouth made him realize that he was biting too hard on the inside of his lip from wanting to scream, or worse, tell Brendan that his make-up looked awful. Silent prayers laced in his eyes, pleading for someone – *anyone* - passing by to step in. Yet not a single kid did. Stares and odd glances were all he was met with, or hurried walks so as to not be caught around the situation.

"Was that some kind of joke? You think I'm gay?" Brendan spat, spittle hitting Kevin's cheek as he held back a grimace, trying to avoid getting hit. Vigorously shaking his head no, Kevin knew not to say anything wrong.

"No! I just wanted to let you know your wig was crooked, I was just trying to be helpful." Kevin explained, doing his best to try and dissolve into the locker. Brendan yanked him forward and then slammed him against the locker again, the sound of it reverberating throughout the hall. This time, it was the back of Kevin's head that took the hit and the pain radiated around the sides until his eyes began to tear. *The term ringing someone's bell was no joke*, he thought, because this was gonna hurt longer than the pain in his back.

"You're not helpful. You're sick. You and all the freaks just like you. I'm sick of all you fags out here lusting after us. This whole school would be better off without you sickos." Brendan snapped again.

Kevin's brain was hurting and he caught the rage in Brendan's gaze as he released one hand from the sequined halter top jumper Kevin was wearing and wrapped it around his throat, squeezing it like a lemon. Panic flooded him and his heart started to race even faster. Unable to breathe, he began clawing at Brendan's long, muscular fingers – trying desperately to get him to let go. Gasping for air as his vision blurred, Kevin barely registered a shadowy figure rushing in from his right before everything went black.

The murmuring of worried voices and the light being shone in his eyes woke Kevin from his nightmare. He was used to them now. Constantly being picked on and bullied was normal for him. But only in his sleep was he ever truly physically hurt - that was until he realized this wasn't one of his nightmares as he blinked, his vision coming into focus. The medicinal smell of the nurse's office and the buzzing around him was a clear indication that it hadn't been a dream. Brendan Moser finally snapped and attacked him. The aching in his throat made him realize he had been choked to the point of passing out.

"Oh, thank God! Kevin, my baby are you okay?" Janie cried, as she pushed aside the paramedic that had been standing over him. Scooping him up into her arms, Kevin sighed as he tried to fight the tears that were threatening to leak out. Janie's squeeze was actually making it slightly difficult to breath, patting his mom on the back she eased off from her smothering. Looking around the room, he saw the audience that had accumulated. Grace, Nurse Diane, two paramedics and for some reason George was standing there with an icepack on his right hand.

"You doing okay there buddy?" George asked. Kevin scanned over George's outfit and realized there was blood on the cheerleading shirt and then it hit him. George had gotten into a fight. Kevin remembered the blur just before he blacked out and realization settled in… George was the one to come to his rescue and clearly had done a number on Brendan. Nodding to George, he felt a sense of relief that someone other than his sister, Nikki and one of his best friends Jim, had his back. He had friends, but none of them would have done what George did.

Walking into the room Vice Principal Murphy, with true concern etched into his normally stern features looked to Kevin and then to George.

"Kevin, are you okay? Your dad is talking to Mr. Calagori now. We need you to come and talk about the incident, if you can. We don't want to rush you, though." The tall man said. Kevin never knew him to be compassionate… he was called the *'Ice Storm'* for a reason. When the students got in trouble, he brought down a rain of icy truths on them and it was pretty fierce. Deep down, Kevin didn't want to talk about it. He wanted to just move on and never speak about it again. But he knew that if he didn't, he would be the victim his whole life.

"I'm okay." Kevin's throat was killing him and his voice scratchy, an obvious result of the choking. As his mother pulled away from him, Kevin slowly sat up feeling like a bug being inspected under a microscope as seven pairs of eyes watched him get up off the bed. Turning to George, Kevin smiled at him and he watched a wave of relief wash over George's face.

"Thank you for saving me." His voice small, but then George flashed him a grin and he felt a little flutter in his chest from the simple response.

"Hey, you did it for me, remember the wig?" George laughed, and it seemed that it was that tiny bit of levity that Kevin needed to keep moving. Smiling to himself, he remembered adjusting George's wig in the parking lot before they had gone into school that morning.

"Mr. Nicols, I am going to need you to come with me as well since you were a witness. We've also called your parents to let them know about the situation." The Vice Principal said, his voice sharper this time. Kevin wasn't sure why the Nicols needed to know, but he was sure everything would be fine. As they headed to the main office, Kevin caught a glimpse of himself. In the reflection of the trophy case of all the awards that the school's teams had won over the years, he finally could see the damage that the school's star wide receiver had done. His throat was now a bright indigo and he could actually make out the finger marks on his neck. Kevin's fingers lightly grazing over the marks along his slender neck his Adam's apple bobbed up and down as he stifled the sob he wanted to let out. Gazing at his reflection he watched as George came up behind him.

"Hey, you are gonna be okay. Even if I have to break his ankle, I will make sure he will never bother you again. I promise." George's voice firm. Kevin wouldn't put it past him. In fact, he was shocked that Brendan wasn't in the nurse's office right alongside of him due to George.

As they got closer to the Principal's office he could hear his father, Ken Cartino, yelling.

"I don't give a shit if he is the President of the United States! He strangled my son! Hang the fucking championship, my child's life was in danger and you mean to tell me that you aren't going to do anything to him simply because he is the star wide receiver? I will sue you, his parents, the school district and the fucking town. That child is an animal!" Ken shouted from behind the closed door. The secretaries sitting in their chairs just exchanged glances at each other and then to Kevin with utter pity in their eyes.

"Mr. Cartino, please calm down, I understand your frustration." The Principal said muffled behind the door. Kevin turned and looked at Janie; her soft eyes had a glint of admiration in them at what was going on behind the door. Moving closer to Kevin, Janie whispered.

"I wouldn't go in there just yet, although I probably should. I'm still not ready to be a widow and one heart attack for him is enough." Janie said, cupping Kevin's face in her palm before moving past him and entering the office leaving Kevin, George and Mr. Murphy standing outside. George walked up to Kevin still holding the icepack on his hand nudging Kevin's shoulder.

"You know, I'm probably gonna get suspended for this." George said, with a slight smile and Kevin couldn't figure out why he would be happy about it.

Before he could respond, the sound of the door to the assistant vice principal's office opening stopped him. Kevin's eyes grew wide and his heart began to race as Brendan Moser, his parents, Coach Foster with Mrs. Hazel stepped out. A wicked sneer spread across Brendan's bruised and bloody face as he started making his way to the doorway. Helplessly frozen in his spot, Kevin couldn't move or even formulate a thought as Brendan approached. Fear coursed through his veins at the thought that Brendan was going to wrap his hands around his throat again until he felt a hand on his shoulder.

Pulling Kevin backwards, within seconds George was standing toe to toe with Brendan. Racing to break the two teammates apart, the two vice principals and Coach Foster scrambled, doing their best to keep the peace and not have a fight right there in the main office. The shouting had stirred enough of a commotion that Kevin's parents and the Principal came running out of his office.

As Kevin stood there watching the entire thing unfold around him, he hadn't realized just how bad things truly were until that moment. Turning to look at his mother for some kind of cue, Janie simply nodded her head towards the door to Mr. Calagori's office and took his hand escorting both him and George in. Before the door shut he watched as two of the security guards escorted Brendan and his parents out of the office.

Taking a deep breath and sitting down across from Mr. Calagori, he knew he would have to explain what exactly happened, and probably all the other times before it. He never said anything before out of fear that the once-a-month occurrence would be worsened if he spoke up. But silence in this case was no longer the answer. Kevin knew that he would go through life constantly fighting the Brendan Moser's of the world, and if he didn't take a stand on it now, then when?

"I can't believe that asshole is only getting detention." Grace said, as Kevin applied more foundation on his neck to cover the bruising. That seemed to be the sentiment everyone was feeling. Every part of his body hurt. His head, throat, and back but mostly his heart more than anything. The fact that Brendan was only getting detention instead of a suspension or expulsion left Kevin feeling like he didn't matter. That not only could anyone just pick on him, but others like him. Because of this, so many other students in school hid who they truly were.

But Kevin was different, he wasn't going to hide anything. His parents taught him that. When he confessed to them that he was interested in boys rather than girls they had not only been supportive - but said they already knew and that they loved him because he was their child and would always be there for him. Kevin thanked God every day for such understanding family and friends. He knew how fortunate he was to have that, unlike so many others who didn't.

Inspecting his handy work, Kevin couldn't seem to stop staring at his neck and despite the fact that he put on what felt like a pound of make-up the bruising still seemed to be there. Walking into the room, Janie smiled at him in the reflection of the mirror and held out the sparkling scarf she held in her hand.

"Here, put this on. It should cover it and not make it so noticeable." Janie said, with a wink. "They should count themselves lucky you weren't more seriously hurt. Daddy is still on a tear about pressing charges against his parents." She added. Whirling around with shock in his deep brown eyes, Kevin knew this would just make things worse.

"Oh God, please don't let him! I just want to move on from this. He is getting punished and hopefully he won't do this again." Kevin sighed. He didn't want anyone making a fuss over the situation.

"*Hopefully,* is nothing more than a dream. But thankfully, with your father being the genius he is, making up that agreement right there on the spot for that mongrel to sign that he wouldn't go anywhere near you or we will press charges should get him to stop. I wish you could've seen Brendan's dad's face." Her eyes widened in delight. "He was so furious and that mouse of a mother just sat there. They didn't even bother to apologize once!" Janie grimaced, as she shook her head in disgust.

Not a single part of that was surprising to him. Kevin knew it was a long shot that the agreement was even going to work. Yet, after all the screaming and yelling his father had done, he was sure that Mr. Moser was not about to want to get into a court case with Ken.

Checking her fake mustache in the mirror, and shoulder bumping Kevin, Grace turned to him with a sweet smile. "Come on Cher, we've got candy baskets to raid. Besides, everyone will be here later for the pizza party around 5 p.m." She said, holding her elbow out for him to take. Grinning warmly down to his sister, he took it, headed down the stairs and out to the street. Without fail every resident in town was there for Basher Avenue trick-or-treating.

Living on Basher Avenue – the most sought-after street for the biggest day of the year – meant that everyone and their brother was there. Five blocks worth of houses were closed off by the town police because of a tradition that started with a simple block party ten years back. He remembered being so young when the tradition started. His parents, as well as a few others secured a permit to have the street blocked off so they could do a huge potluck and so that the kids could enjoy themselves on Halloween night. One block, turned into two, and by year five the entire town just seemed to only want to go to Basher Avenue. The stories about this block party spread like wildfire, and within the past year people from other towns in the area were now trick-or-treating there as well, making parking on the side streets impossible.

With the warm weather, the town let all the owners on Basher Avenue know that they would be setting up a patrol station in the middle in case there were any public disturbances and for crowd control. After the events at school, Kevin thought of just staying in, but this was his second favorite holiday and he wasn't going to miss it.

Scanning the dense crowd of every age dressed in costumes, Grace yanked his arm and motioned towards the epicenter of the chaos. Directly in the busiest intersection of it all, was one of the SWAT trucks and a bunch of officers passing out candy and glow necklaces to anyone wanting free goodies. But there was just one officer he hadn't recognized before until they turned around. George's cheerleader costume was now replaced with a delicious looking police uniform triggering Kevin's heart to flutter. A slight tingling ran up his spine, his feet slightly faltering as he approached. Kevin watched as Grace ran up to George giving him a huge hug, and a small knot in his stomach twisted as he just stood there watching it unfold. His mind raced. *What is happening? Is Grace now dating George since she broke up with Jimmy again? Why am I turned on by George wearing a costume? Oh my God, please dick don't get hard right now! Mom and Dad kissing, Mom and Dad kissing, golf, tennis, all of the sports.* Taking a deep breath in, he kept moving towards George and just prayed he could keep his teenage hormones in check. Kevin had never seen George dressed as a police officer before and all he could think was that if George were ever to become one, Kevin may want to take up a life of crime just so he could be handcuffed by him.

"Hey there pal, how you holding up?" George asked, placing Grace down on the ground and flashing that brilliant white smile. Kevin shrugged. he was fine until he saw him in that outfit - *not that he'd ever admit that out loud.*

"I'm okay. You changed?" Kevin said, looking everywhere but at George as he silently hoped he wouldn't notice the way he avoided his gaze.

"Oh yeah, well with me being part of the D.A.R.E. program, I volunteered to help pass out candy, so figured I would dress up as a cop. Luckily, one of the sergeants is the same size as me and let me borrow it for just the day. Technically I'm not supposed to wear this, but chief signed off on it." George said, smiling down at all the kids and adding candy into their buckets. Nodding, Kevin kept averting his gaze and it seemed to catch Grace's notice.

"Alright, Kevin and I are gonna keep going. Will you and your parents be by later?" She asked, causing Kevin's heart to flutter again. Even though he was grateful to George for saving him earlier, he was really having a difficult time looking at him all dressed up in that uniform. But it didn't stop him from looking up from the ground, that little bit of nosiness wanting to catch George's response.

"Yeah, Mom and Dad didn't punish me for getting suspended, so we will be there. I have to remember to thank your mom again for the invite." George grinned again as he opened another bag of glow necklaces to pass out. His eyes never leaving George's face, Grace cleared her throat and whisked Kevin away before he made a complete fool of himself. Once they were a safe distance away and doing their best to avoid other trick-or-treaters from knocking them over, Grace stopped short.

"He isn't your type, you know." The sadness in Grace's voice conveyed what she was trying to say.

"I know, but it doesn't mean that I can't look at the menu." Kevin smirked.

"Oh, look away! I just don't want you getting your hopes up." Grace reached down into her bag finding a piece of candy and shoving it into her mouth.

"You aren't jealous that I would look at him?" Kevin asked as a princess bumped into him. Glancing around, he realized they were holding up traffic and needed to keep moving.

"Why would I be jealous? It's not like I'm dating him." Grace shoved another piece of candy in her mouth and waved at someone she knew.

"I thought with that hug you guys had started dating since you broke up with –." Kevin stopped short of saying Jimmy's name knowing it would break her heart. Grace's depression was bad enough that she was in therapy once a week since the incident. So, the fact that she had even ventured out of the house was a huge deal.

"No, it's just that I have a lot to be thankful for with George, that's all." Grace said. The sound of feet stomping on the ground from behind them made both Grace and Kevin turn as Nikki came bounding up dressed up like a zombie princess.

"So, what candy did you two bitches get? I must have hit most of the houses that were giving out crappy hard candy and pennies. Who gives pennies?" Nikki said, jiggling her bag to the sound of the pennies rustling around at the bottom. As they looked in their bags, Nikki, Grace and Kevin were getting shoved around by all the people on the streets. It wasn't until Kevin smelt the heavy cologne in the air that he spun around to see Brendan Moser and two of the other football players walking behind them. His heart stopped and once again he felt himself slipping into the frozen state of fear, unable to move or speak. Within an instant, Grace and Nikki ran in front of him and despite their tremendous size difference, they showed absolutely no fear.

"Back the fuck up, dipshit. You already got one beating today. You wanna get another one?" Nikki yelled, hands on her hips and not backing down. Brendan looked her up and down giving the impression that he was unchanged by her or her attitude.

"You need to get the hell away from us. You signed an agreement and as you can see we have *plenty* of witnesses, and oh, look the police are right over there. So, how about you tuck your dick up your ass where you like it and get fucking moving!" Grace smugly added to Nikki's threat.

Kevin was astonished at the gumption and tenacity of his sister and her best friend. The guys in front of them were monsters, well over a foot taller than both of them. Yet there they were, ready to go head-to-head with them. *One day*, he thought, *one day he would be brave enough to stand up and fight his own battle*. His eyes darted towards the parents and other kids in the area looking on at the exchange and noticed one of the school secretaries walking over with her granddaughter.

"Well, didn't I see you all enough today? Mr. Moser, Mr. Ngyuen, Mr. Blake, I believe you all should go finish trick-or-treating. In fact, Mr. Moser, considering your actions earlier today, I'm shocked your parents even let you out of the house and I would hate to inform Mr. Calagori, Coach Foster and Mr. Cartino that you violated your agreement. Not only would you not be able to play, but you would be expelled, and I'm sure that will not look good to any potential colleges looking at your records for scholarship. Now would it?" The elderly woman said. Kevin's heart rate seemed to ease as he watched Brendan's bruised face turn into a scowl. There was never a more perfect time for Mrs. Locke to show up and be nosey than right this second.

"We're leaving. The candy is crap here anyway." Brendan said, turning around and heading in the other direction. Mrs. Locke turned, smiling at Kevin and the girls.

"Some kids just never learn. You go off and have a good time. Come Evie, Gammy wants some Snickers." The older woman turned to her tiny grand-daughter and then motioned to two young men that were finishing a conversation with another couple. As the young men approached they chatted and laughed.

"Charlie, Carl, these are three students from my school. This is Grace, Nicole and Kevin. Kevin had a run-in earlier today with someone, something like what you went through Charlie. Kids, this is my son, Charles, his partner Carl and their daughter, my beautiful granddaughter Evie." Mrs. Locke said, beaming with pride.

At that very moment Kevin suddenly understood. Before him stood not just a woman or a secretary, but a grandmother, a mom, but first and foremost - an ally. This family in front of him was his dream. That one day he would find his soul mate and be able to live a long happy life. As he watched Carl pick up his daughter, the sting of tears begging to free themselves from Kevin's eyes stirred him to blink. Charlie's warm, caring smile let him know he understood exactly what he was feeling. Charlie could relate to what he had gone through, but something in his gaze made Kevin realize that there would still be more for years to come. As he watched the silent exchange between the two grown men, he knew. There was hope that one day he would find his person.

CHAPTER ONE

George

September 2025

George went into the ball bag and handed Hank the item he previously hid for him. Stepping away from the backstop, heading to the other side of the dugout to watch it all unfold. Tossing his mitt onto the ground, Hank got down on one knee so that he wasn't blocking the plate and as Denise rounded third and was halfway down the baseline she came to a sudden halt, realizing what was happening. George erupted into laughter as the crowd cheered and screamed. He couldn't have been happier for his friends at this very moment. Both of them coming such a long way and here they were just a year later getting engaged.

"What are you doing?" Denise asked, her eyes filled with tears as she approached.

"Denise Gagnon, I have spent years of my life not sure who I was or what I wanted to be. I thought I was perfect, but you have challenged me from the very moment I met you. You have pushed me, you yelled at me, you hated me, but all of it was warranted. But then something happened, something I never expected ever in my life. You gave me the one thing I thought I could never find in a partner. Love. No one except my own boys has ever truly given that to me. You not only love me, but you showed me that I was worthy of it. That with all my darkness, all my insecurities, I deserve love. And so do you. I don't want anyone else in this entire world but you. So, I am asking, *NO begging you*, in front of all our friends and family, I'm pleading for you to be my wife." Hank asked.

George had to hand it to him. That was a damn good proposal and considering how Denise was, she deserved it. These two had been through Hell and back, with their past lives and now together. But he was truly happy for them. Despite the two of them being at odds with one another because of George and Denise's relationship, it meant a lot to him that Hank asked for his help with setting the entire proposal up.

As he observed the whispered exchange between them, he knew by the look on Hank's face she had said '*yes*' and watched on as they kissed. George's heart swelled with joy for them, but as he watched so many other couples embracing a part of his ached as well. For George there was no one. All he had were his friends, Maybe it was time to get that dog he was contemplating about getting. At least someone would be happy to spend the rest of their life with him. But he wasn't going to dwell. His friends had found their person and they would live happily ever after.

"Are we all still heading to the Sun for drinks after?" Kevin asked, in between screaming and cheering. George just nodded his head. *Everyone paired off as usual, now I know how Bridget Jones felt,* he thought to himself. And that thought struck him, before Kevin moved in he would never even watch that movie and now he could recite it by heart with the amount of times they watched it. Chuckling to himself, George realized that there were a lot of things that he had never done or watched before Kevin moved in.

"Yeah, I am gonna go now and get everything set up." George said, watching as everyone went running over to Denise and Hank to celebrate. It was a beautiful moment, but for him just another reminder of what he was missing. He caught the look of concern on Kevin's face and there was no denying he was pitying him.

Heading over to his car, George thought perhaps it was better he wasn't in a relationship; his job was so much a part of him and very few people understood that. Kevin did, but that was only because he was his roommate. The past few dates that George had been on, the women mentioned wanting to find someone who could dedicate more time to them. But if given the opportunity, George would always take overtime so he could save. He didn't want to live in the condo forever. His dream was to get a house near a lake and just be able to go fishing and have a bonfire with his favorite music playing in the background. It was simple, peaceful and quiet. He has enough nieces and nephews to enjoy them. And to be honest at forty-seven years old, he really wasn't interested in changing diapers and wanting to start a family this late. Unless the right person came along and was young enough to handle an old man and children to take care of.

As he turned the truck on, he pulled out of the spot and proceeded to the Sun. Honestly, all he wanted was to go home or be at work. The last date he went on had been at the Sun and it ended horribly. Although, it was sweet of Jonathan to set him up with his hairdresser friend, she was only looking for a sugar daddy and while she was pretty, he just wasn't into younger women. He didn't want some large age gap between himself and his partner. A few years, sure. But he wanted someone he could make jokes with about stuff from the 80s and 90s who would get the references and not have to explain it.

Pulling up to the light next to Nico's Bar and Grill, something in their window caught his eye. Kevin's boyfriend, Jonathan, was sitting at a table right in the center with another man. The younger blonde-haired gentleman was the stark contrast of his roommate. Kevin had become so distinguished looking as he grew older. Kevin's younger self's obsidian black hair had started to gray at the temples, and he always joked about his smile lines, but George just laughed, because in his mind, he only saw the young man he went to school with. Watching, Jonathan wiped something off of the younger man's lip and sucked it off his thumb. Solid move. George himself had done that a few times to women and it landed them in his bed. *Was he cheating on Kevin? Did Kevin agree to an open relationship after all?* George thought as he watched the younger man blush, his heart pounding in his chest with anger for his friend.

HONK! The light turned green and the car behind him blew its horn, stirring enough of a ruckus that the people in the window turned to look. George locked eyes with Jonathan. Panic and shock spread across Jonathan's face, and it said everything that George needed to know. Yet, not wanting to anger the drivers behind him much longer, he kept going until he got into The Sun's parking lot. Sitting there his chest burns, something rumbled deep under his ribs. It was nothing he ever felt before and a small part of him was scared. His normally calm demeanor was gone, as he took a deep breath in he felt the heated anger start to wash over him.

"What the fuck is wrong with this guy?" George mumbled, thinking about how Kevin was going to react to Jonathan cheating on him. Although, there was no actual proof. Taking in another deep breath, that pesky investigator side of him took hold. He needed to remain calm and try to analyze the situation. They could have just been friends meeting each other and overly affectionate with one another. Kevin himself was that way with him. Kevin's nickname for George was Big Sexy, which originally was odd, but it was just a term of endearment. Kevin was nothing but sweet, loving, and funny. The list could go on and on, but he also had his faults. He was an awful gossip, terrible flirt, and recited lines from movies while actually watching the movie. George's heart ached for him knowing that this was going to destroy his friend again.

Taking a deep breath, he tried to gather himself so he could take care of business. Getting out of the truck he made his way into the restaurant looking for the hostess and didn't seem to see her. Popping his head over into the large bar area, he walked over to the elderly, curly red-haired woman who was his Kindergarten teacher's assistant all those years ago.

"Hey Mrs. Riggi, is Caroline here? We're gonna be having a big group coming in from the softball game and we have a celebration so we need as many tables as possible." George said. The smile the bloomed across the tiny woman's face glowed.

"OH! Did Denise say yes? Oh, I am so glad!!!" Annie Riggi cheered, clasping her hands and running from behind the bar to hug George. "Yes, Caroline is just getting all the tables set up. Oh, I'm so glad it worked out, I know you are next! I can feel it." Her smile and joy overflowing so much that he didn't have it in his heart to tell her different.

"From your lips to God's ears, right?" George smiled, pulling her in for a hug. As the large wooden door creaked open he turned casting his eyes on someone he hadn't seen in years. There stood what looked like a beaten down, balding, heavier, younger version of Brendan Moser's dad. George's eyes widened as he realized this wasn't his dad, it WAS Brendan Moser. The years were clearly not kind to him. The once young, handsome, talented man he was no longer stood in the doorframe of the bar in front of him.

"Holy shit, Brendan?" George questioned, an embarrassed shock grew across the other man's face as he realized who he was standing in front of.

"Oh my God, George? George Nicols? How the heck are ya? It's been what – thirty years?" Brendan's voice garbled under what sounded like years of heavy smoking. George's mom had told him while he was in the Marines that Brendan suffered a massive ACL injury in his junior year of college and apparently it was bad enough that the injury sunk any hopes Brendan had for his professional football career. Willing to let bygones be bygones, George extended his hand and shook Brendan's.

"I've been well. Thanks for asking. How've you been? I heard you moved out of Toselle Park. Are you just visiting?" George was just trying to be polite as he asked. Brendan rubbed the top of his head where there used to be a full head of hair and grimaced.

"Uh, no. I just moved back in with my parents. My ex took everything in the divorce, the bitch. So now I'm reduced to living with my folks and need to get a job." Brendan explained. George did his very best not to feel slightly happy that someone who had been absolutely horrible to people in his youth was finally getting his karmic justice. Doing his best to look understanding of a terrible situation, he just nodded but inside he wanted to laugh.

"What about you?" Brendan asked again, this time looking at George's left hand and seemed to notice that he didn't have a wedding ring. "Never got married or divorced?" Brendan questioned. Absentmindedly wringing his hands, George just smiled.

"Married to my career, so neither." Again, that tiny ache in his heart pulsed. It wasn't that he didn't want to be married or in a relationship. It was just that he hadn't found his person. Behind Brendan a commotion started in the vestibule of the restaurant and he recognized the voices. As the gang finally arrived, it was like the universe knew exactly when to save him.

"Well, it was great catching up but my party is here, so let me go. Big celebration. Hope to see you again soon." George said, lying through his teeth. If he never saw him again that would be wonderful, however, now that Brendan was back George was sure in a tiny town like Toselle Park, it was sadly bound to happen. Patting Brendan's shoulder, George made his way to the group converging on The Sun Porch.

As they all raised their glasses in honor of Denise and Hank, George looked around at the amazing group of friends he got to share his life with. Thankful after all these years to have reconnected again he smiled as they all laughed and joked.

He and Kevin, however, had always stayed friends even when he went into the Marines. Then when he joined the force, it was George that suggested to hire Kevin to build the town's website and use him to DJ any of the retirement parties for the officers that were leaving the force. However, despite their little group seeming to have everyone paired off, he never felt alone. Jim became his running buddy, Hank and Kevin went with him to the gym and Mike had asked him to volunteer with coaching the boys football team over the course of the summer due to one of the teacher's having retired at the end of the year.

For so many years George had kept to himself, dedicating his life to his career, hoping one day he would find someone who would be so interesting that he would instantly want to devote more time to them rather than his job. Yet no one materialized from this fantastical dream he played in his head.

He would be in a crowded bar - people would be elbow to elbow - when a person would bump into his back. He would turn, and a raven-haired faceless person would be standing there. And through the loud noises around them a garbled inaudible *"hi"* was all that was said between them. In every dream his heart would race and he'd wake up with a smile knowing that one day he would find this mystery person.

The clinking of spoons to glasses brought him back to reality as he blinked to watch Denise and Hank kiss. George felt a tiny twang in the pit of his stomach as it had just been a year before that he and Denise were dating. In truth, it had been fun, but that was all. Fun. Laughing at the gagging noises Jodi and Calvin were making, he decided to excuse himself to head to the bathroom.

Walking through the bar making his way to the restrooms, he looked toward the other side of the bar to see Brendan sitting there by himself, nursing what looked like his second beer. George hadn't talked to him since senior year and it seemed just from that tiny conversation that Brendan wasn't having the easiest time lately. Divorce was complicated, he learned that between his sister, Bernadette and then what he saw between his friends. Which made him realize just how fortunate he had been not to find somebody at this point. He was a workaholic. George would never deny it, but perhaps if he found someone he enjoyed spending time with it might change his mind.

Finishing his business and washing his hands, on his way back to the table he looked up to find Kevin heading his way with a bit of a panic on his face.

"Um, you are not gonna believe who is at our table right now talking to Grace, Nikki, and Jim like they are their best friend." Kevin said so quickly that a normal person who didn't know Kevin-speed wouldn't have understood what had just been said. Sighing, George turned his head towards the bar area and saw that Brendan was no longer in his seat and with the panic etched on Kevin's face, instantly knew.

"I saw him earlier. Apparently, he is recently divorced and living in town." George explained, and Kevin just rolled his eyes.

"Good for his wife, bad for us." Kevin huffed followed by an elongated sigh. "I know I'm not fifteen anymore and I can stand up for myself, but what is it about this guy? Like I have a great life. I have an amazing job… well, jobs, but all I have are you guys and Jonathan." Kevin gushed. And then George remembered Jonathan and that young man at Nico's. He still wasn't sure exactly what to do. Did he tell Kevin and break his heart? Or did he give Jonathan the benefit of the doubt and ask him for an explanation without involving Kevin? "I'm just in a really good place right now, I can't let this guy ruin everything."

The pain of years past mirrored in Kevin's deep brown eyes tearing at George's heart. He knew Kevin well enough to know that he was heading to the bathroom to escape. They could easily sneak around the bar and just go out the front door knowing that the hostess station blocked the view of the door from where the tables were situated. But that wouldn't be very adult of them. Closing his eyes, George formulated a plan in his brain, but he wasn't sure he could do it. But it would keep Brendan off of Kevin's back for good, he hoped.

"You can't run from him forever, but I have a plan. Do you trust me?" George asked, still hesitant at what he was going to do. Kevin just shook his head and George was slightly offended until Kevin said, "With my life? Like it's a question? Of course I trust you."

Grabbing Kevin's hand, George calmly walked him back to the table. This needed to work. Steeling himself against any hesitation that George had from the odd feelings he would occasionally get whenever Kevin would do something that triggered them, George found a new determination to go into protector mode. This was his friend. Kevin had been hurt by this person before, both physically and mentally, and George was not going to allow this to happen in Kevin's adult life.

Approaching the table, he watched as Brendan's eyes focused on Kevin who had been hesitantly trailing behind George. Tightening his grip on Kevin's hand, George's heart raced, he was doing this to protect Kevin. If Jonathan wasn't going to be here to stand by Kevin and he was going to cheat on him with some younger guy, then someone needed to stand next to him. And if that meant that George was the one to do it, then he was going to protect his friend at all cost.

"Well, well, look who we have here? How's it going?" Brendan sneered, looking Kevin up and down, and George felt Kevin shift behind him. *If Kevin was going to stand up to Brendan, he needed to not revert back to being that fifteen-year-old self,* George thought. Turning his head back to Kevin, George flashed a wink to him so only he could see. Kevin furrowed his brow ever so slightly and it seemed that he still didn't know what to do. George pulled Kevin in next to him, squeezing his hand again to give him some confidence. With a shuddered sigh, Kevin seemed to find the confidence he needed and smiled back at Brendan.

"Fine. I'm fine." Kevin stuttered. Brendan's devious grin grew wider and a heated anger suddenly hit George. The man in front of them hadn't changed. George had seen predators before and that was the look and movement of one. Releasing Kevin's hand, George slipped his arm around Kevin's waist and smiled at Brendan and then smiled at Kevin doing his best to give him a loving look. *This needs to work,* George thought.

"Oh, come on, *Babe.* You don't have to be so modest." George said, his eyes focused on Kevin trying to relay his thoughts all in one look. Sadly, this was not one of those times. Turning his head back to

Brendan, the look of astonishment made George laugh just a little, even though he was getting the message and it only made George pull Kevin closer.

"Kevin is just so shy about all the great things he can do. I know he hates when I talk about how amazing he is, so I won't embarrass him. Right *Babe*?" George said, and it seemed Kevin finally got it. Wrapping his arm around George's waist, George could feel Kevin relax just a little more and even his posture straightened. As Kevin flashed a brilliant, relieved smile to George, an odd tingle shimmered at the base of his spine. There was something about that tiny gesture. Kevin's closeness and his smile caused George to question this reaction from his own body. Especially one from Kevin.

It was brief, but he found himself looking into Kevin's eyes and not just finding relief, but a peace. George had never been this close to Kevin. His eyes were almost a chocolate brown, like a deep chocolate cup of cocoa. George blinked because that tingle was starting back up again in his spine and he wasn't sure why. Tearing himself away, he faced Brendan and the rest of the table. Grace, Nikki and Denise were doing their best not to laugh, while the rest of the guys all seemed confused. But the best reaction to all this was Brendan's.

Shaking his head, Brendan appeared to be confused. "Wait a minute, you two are together?" Brendan asked in utter astonishment.

"Sure." George said. *It wasn't a confirmation per se. It was more of a I'll let you think that you buffoon,* George thought.

"Oh, *Sweetie,* I forgot we need to stop on our way home and pick up milk. We are all out, I used the last of it with my breakfast." Kevin added with a smile. It was taking everything in George not to laugh as the expression on Brendan's face was priceless. Blinking rapidly at the *"reality"* that was standing in front of him, Brendan just kept shaking his head and his eyes seemed to dart between George and Kevin, only making the protective creature that lived deep in George's chest roar with laughter. *That's right, you will never mess with him ever again.*

"Uh, uh, well uh." Brendan stuttered, completely at a loss for words. "Really? You two?" he asked.

"Yeah, you got a problem with that douchebag?" Denise chimed in from the table, as Grace bit her bottom lip to keep from laughing. Brendan whipped his head around not realizing that there were other people still there. Disgusted, he pointed to George and Kevin, Brendan didn't seem to be buying it and George needed to act fast. He needed him to leave them alone for good.

"George is straight. He's always been straight, right?" Brendan exclaimed, his voice a whole octave higher.

"Is this guy for real? You knew him when, in high school? Dude you know that most people don't figure out who they are till the hormones start to chill, right? Seriously, were you friends with this guy?" Denise asked. Brendan turned and glared at her, still not believing any of what was being said.

"There is no way you two are together! I don't believe it." Brendan uttered, his face now red with embarrassment at being told off. George needed to act and act fast. This conversation should have been over already but it seemed that Brendan was just as dense as he was back in high school. *It seemed someone never matured,* George thought. He knew he was gonna have to bite a bullet on it and hopefully this would all end right here and now.

Bringing Kevin closer to him, George looked at his friend and roommate and prayed he would understand that this was just a show. This was to protect him so that Brendan would never bother Kevin again. If there was anyone who Brendan should go after, it should be him, not Kevin. George knew that Brendan would never attempt harm on him, for fear of retaliation.

Staring into his friend's eyes he took a deep breath and did the one thing he never thought he would ever do. Closing his eyes George gently brushed his lips against Kevin's. They were softer than he expected, plump and warm, almost welcoming… and his head wasn't sure this was actually the right thing to do. Their breath mingled and it warmed every cell of George's body. The sound of Brendan gasping spurred George on. *Convincing, this needs to be convincing,* he thought and then kissed Kevin right there in front of everyone.

It was quick, just to shut Brendan up, it didn't mean anything. What was just supposed to be a quick peck on the lips, turned into something a bit longer. The lips touching his were inviting and for a second George forgot it was Kevin as a warmth stirred in his chest. George's hand pressed against Kevin's back moving him closer and a tiny sigh escaped his lips as something deep within stirred him to want to deepen the kiss. But the huffing sound of disgust pulled him back to reality. As George opened his eyes he saw something in Kevin's that kept him still close and unable to break away. George didn't know what it was and he wasn't sure why his own heart's rhythm was all off, but in his mind he prayed this little show worked, because this odd feeling from their kiss made him a bit woozy. Kevin's rapid blinking clearly indicated that he was slightly weirded out, but whatever was going on was suddenly broken by the continued disgusted sound coming from Brendan.

"Ugh, you two are freaks, I'm out." Brendan spat as he stormed out of the room. Smiling as he watched Brendan stomp off, George turned back to the shocked crowd sitting at the table.

"And I wasn't even in theater with you guys. I guess that worked." George said, trying to regain himself and his faculties. Kevin, however, was still doing his rapid eye blinking. "You okay there pal? I think he is finally gonna leave you alone." George said, waving his hand in front of Kevin's face until his eyes focused. Kevin's brow furrowed again and he shot Grace a quick glance. George knew this look. After years of their friendship, Kevin and Grace could have a silent conversation just with looks.

"Kev, he will leave you alone, I promise." George's tone this time was not as light as it normally as, making sure Kevin understood. He would take the brunt of whatever backlash this would cause because this was Kevin, and he was his friend.

CHAPTER TWO

Kevin

The air and space around him seemed to be swirling. *Did that really just happen?* Still reeling from George's kiss, Kevin tried to focus on his words, anything but the strange feelings in his heart. He knew it didn't mean anything. It was just his friend defending him - protecting him. *St. George to the rescue again*, Kevin thought. But even though that kiss had no true meaning behind it, why did his head become so fuzzy? It was almost as if all words and comprehension were not even possible.

An aching emptiness filled him the moment he pulled himself away from the tall, hard, broad body that held him close. After all this time, years of that boyish crush for George appeared to be creeping back into his heart. But his head suddenly came into focus and it was screaming. *Oh God, Jonathan!* With Brendan suddenly showing up starting issues again, Kevin had completely forgotten all about his partner. How was he going to explain this to Jonathan? He just needed to remember, it wasn't real, it was just so that Brendan would leave him alone.

Watching George take his seat, Kevin seemed unable to move from where he was standing. Spying Jim's gaze, his eyes widened hoping that Jim would recognize how he was feeling and needed to escape. Fortunately for him, Jim indeed spoke Kevin, took one quick sip of his beer before he got up from his seat.

"Hey, you want to step outside and get some air there, tiger?" Jim asked. Silently nodding Kevin let himself be pulled away from the crowd.

"Where are you two going?" Grace yelled after them.

"I need to complain about you, so I'm stealing your brother. If I complain about you to Nikki she'll kick my ass." Jim yelled back. Kevin laughed but he knew the truth, Jim worshipped the ground Grace walked on so he wouldn't have a single thing to complain about. However, even after years of being away from the group, Jim could still read him like a book. The only thing Kevin wondered about was if he still remembered him confessing back in high school that he had a crush on George?

"Damn right! Besides, Kevin is gonna tell me anyway." Nikki screamed, as the conversations behind them seemed to turn into tiny murmurs as they headed out the front door. With Jim leading the way, he pulled Kevin over to the outdoor bar and sat him down. Kevin's mind was everywhere and yet nowhere all at the same time.

"Well, that was unexpected." Jim looked down at Kevin and all he could do was continue to blink. Running his fingers through his dark wavy hair, Kevin tried to calm his brain. Remembering his yoga classes with Denise, Kevin stretched out his arms and raised them above his head. Taking a deep breath in with one fluid motion breathed out, "FUUUUUUUUCK!"

Jim laughed and Kevin would have too if his brain wasn't a hot mess. Covering his mouth with both hands, Kevin knew that there was so much more he needed to get out and Jim skeptically looked down at him.

"You want to let the rest of them out? I know you better than Nikki does. Don't tell her that. She thinks she is your bestie but go ahead." Jim said, pulling up a chair preparing for the unleashing of all the cursing.

"What the fuck? What the fuck? What the fuckity fuckery fuck was that?" Kevin screeched, still running his hands through his hair and then rubbing his face.

"You done?" Jim asked, almost knowing there was more.

"How? How? How am I supposed to face George? I live with him? How am I supposed to keep dating Jonathan? I just kissed my best friend -" Kevin exclaimed.

"Hey, I take offense to that. I thought I was your best friend." Jim said, looking rather dejected at the idea that someone else was Kevin's best friend.

"Best friend that I live with. How am I supposed to go and act like nothing happened? Does he know I had a crush on him a million years ago? I can't tell him. He will kick me out!" Kevin's exasperation drenched in the high-pitched tone. Jim frowned, reaching over to Kevin, gripping his shoulder trying to ease the tension that seemed to be knitting itself with the weight of this new situation. Kevin wasn't sure what he was going to do. How was it that after all these years, one single fake kiss would suddenly cause him to get so flustered? Kevin knew it was just for show, it didn't mean anything.

"He isn't gonna kick you out. You and I both know that it was just to make Brendan go away." Jim consoled, but for some reason that tiny mention that it hadn't meant anything, made a pang in Kevin's heart he couldn't understand. He knew they were just friends, that was the zone in which George kept him in and that was fine. But it didn't make the pain of never being seen as anything more hurt any less. Taking in another deep breath, Kevin rolled his head trying to relax his neck and shoulders.

"I don't know what to do." Kevin said, closing his eyes, wishing that he could have just been brave enough to have faced Brendan without anyone having to come to his aid. He was a grown ass man, and there he was, still feeling like the helpless fifteen-year-old. Leaning further back into the chair, he put his head back and opened his eyes to look up to the sky. The sun was setting and the sky was that pretty pink with just a hint of inky blue as it was finally turning to night.

"There is nothing to do. You are gonna go in and celebrate your friends getting engaged. You are gonna thank your friend for being supportive and you are gonna go on and have a wonderful relationship with Jonathan and live happily ever after with him." Jim said, almost like a command rather than an explanation. "Unless." He added, almost like a question.

"Unless? Unless what?" Kevin snapped his head up and looked back to Jim, whose half-cocked smile gave Kevin a queasy feeling in his stomach.

"Unless you want that kiss to mean more or shall I say *be* more." Jim said. There it was. The crux of all of Kevin's issues in his heart and head right that second. Shaking his head over and over, Kevin didn't want to think or better yet hope that it could be.

"No." Kevin replied, softly resigning himself that single feeling. "No, I am with Jonathan. George is just my friend and he only did that to help me out. That is it. I -" Kevin paused. He thought of all the countless straight men he had met and all the crushes there were over the years - George being just one of many – that he would never get the chance to be with. Realistically he knew there was no chance with George, even if that part of his heart that had been locked away for years recently decided to resurface. George was straight – Kevin didn't stand a chance.

"I am just going to enjoy my friends." Kevin resigned, and deep in his heart, that tiny space he always held for George broke once again.

"Okay, well then that is that. But if you need to chat again, you know where to find me." Jim said, getting up from his chair helping Kevin up. Looking up at his brother-in-law, Kevin felt a little better, or at least better than he was before he headed outside. Hugging Jim actually seemed to ease the tension. As far as older brother-in-laws went, Jim was the best he could have ever asked for. And although Grace was a great older sister and gave the sweetest hugs, Jim's were notoriously the best.

"Thank you. Have I mentioned just how happy I am at how things with you and Grace worked out… well minus the whole psycho ex-wife thing. But just having you here in our lives again." Kevin paused, smiling to Jim. "I'm just so glad that things worked out in the end." Kevin said, as they made their way back into the restaurant. Jim snickered and bobbed his head in agreement.

"Yeah, well sometimes life is funny that way. You think you are gonna have life go one way and then the universe says hold my beer." Jim said, as he patted Kevin on the back and headed into the restaurant to join their friends.

The warmth of the water on his face felt almost cool. The memory of the kiss ran through his mind and Kevin was trying very hard not to think about it. But every time he touched his lips he could feel George's on them. They had been so gentle, nothing like any other kiss he previously experienced. Standing there inspecting his reflection, his cheeks were flushed and the rosy hue was his dead giveaway that these feelings were going to be more difficult to fight. As he finished his evening routine of facial care, he turned to the tiny knock on the door to the bathroom.

Standing in the doorframe George looked more delicious with his night clothes on. Trying his best to be as nonchalant as always, Kevin allowed his eyes to slowly gaze over the figure standing in the door. George was wearing a loose-fitting pair of lounge pants and tank top that was doing nothing to cover up the muscular chest and arms that he had worked so hard for at the gym. Swallowing hard, Kevin couldn't help but feel that familiar tightening in his balls and a surge of warmth spreading through his chest at the sight of his roommate.

"Is that a new moisturizer?" George asked, his voice soft as he moved into the bathroom making his way over to the sink. Kevin didn't know what to do, George never asked about his skin care.

"Uh, yeah how did you know?" Kevin asked, unsure of where this was going.

"I can smell the hint of lavender; your normal one doesn't have that." George said, taking the bottle out of Kevin's hand, his fingers grazing Kevin's and that tiny touch seemed to feel like a feather dusting his skin, sending chills running up his arm.

"You know what my moisturizers smell like?" Kevin asked. This didn't seem right as he watched George open the cap to the bottle and inhaled the calming lavender scent. George's eyes closed and made a tiny "*mmm*" sound enjoying the aroma. Kevin's heart fluttered at the moan and felt a slight twitch from his dick as it started to get hard and he prayed that George wouldn't notice.

"I know exactly what you smell like, I just didn't know what you tasted like before." George said, stalking up to Kevin and he didn't know what to do. He took a step back toward the wall of the bathroom as George took another step closer.

"Tasted like?" Kevin stuttered, his heart slamming in his chest as his back finally landed against the bathroom wall. He had nowhere to go as George was mere inches away. He felt caged and he didn't know if he liked it or if he was going to cry out of fear. George's eyes cast over Kevin's face and then he reached up brushing his thumb along Kevin's jaw line trailing down to his chin. George's strong hands felt like nothing more than a whisper as Kevin felt his chin being lifted up and George lowered his face closer to his.

"Yes, taste. Your lips must taste like something. I already knew they were soft, but I couldn't taste them before." George whispered, his face hovering so close and Kevin realized he was at full hard-on. With George's nearness he couldn't hide it. He was speechless and frozen as George lowered his head and his lips touched his again. This time it was faint, like a memory just out of reach. Kevin wanted more, needed more. Throwing caution to the wind, Kevin wrapped his arms around George's neck and kissed him properly and to his utter delight it was returned. He felt George's arms wind around his waist and squeeze him tight pulling his body close and to his surprise, he wasn't the only one aroused.

Only, he couldn't quite make out the size. His brain was fuzzy from the intensity of George's kisses as his tongue teased at Kevin's bottom lip and it felt off. George pulled away from his lips and started kissing down his chin, then to his jaw.

"Kevin." George uttered, soft and sweet. But for some reason there was a slight buzzing noise somewhere in the background but Kevin surrendered to the kisses on his neck.

"Kevin." George said, again this time not so sweet and for some reason that buzzing noise seemed to get louder. George pulled away from his neck looking deep in Kevin's eyes.

"Kevin, your alarm is going off." George said, and the spell was broken.

Blinking to the bright light of day, Kevin's sight was not as clear, and he realized that the buzzing noise was indeed his alarm. He wasn't in the bathroom, he was laying in his bed and George was fully dressed in his uniform standing over him looking rather concerned.

"Hey, you okay? Your alarm has been going off for the past minute." George said, his gaze concerned and not like the George that was just in his dream. Scrambling to grab his phone to turn off the alarm and his glasses so he could see, Kevin could feel his morning wood and tried covering it up so that George didn't notice, but it seemed he did as he laughed.

"Kev, I'm a dude. It happens to me too, so don't worry. I just wanted to make sure you were alright. I'm heading out, but are you gonna be okay?" George questioned. Kevin wasn't sure if he was. But he wasn't about to confess that he just woke him from a dream about them making out.

"Yeah, I'm fine. Probably too much to drink last night." Kevin said. He knew he needed to talk to Jim or Grace or both at this point. If only they hadn't kissed, he would not be reliving these feelings that he buried years ago.

George's skeptical gaze was making Kevin feel uncomfortable as he shifted again in his bed. He just needed George to leave so he could get up and hop into a cold shower after that dream. Taking his phone and finally turning off the alarm, Kevin noticed a missed text from Jonathan. In all the insanity of the alarm, dream, and the kiss from the night before, he had forgotten to reach out to him and Kevin knew he was going to get pissy if he didn't.

"Alright, well drink some water." George said, looking down at his watch. "Shit, I'm gonna be late. Take it easy today and I'll see ya later." George said, turning and leaving. Taking in a deep breath the moment he heard the front door shut, Kevin was finally able to breathe. A part of him wanted to go back to sleep but was now completely terrified he would have another dream about his roommate. Instead, he texted Jonathan to see how the interview with the new stylist had gone the night before, anything to switch his frame of mind onto something other than himself.

It seemed that Jonathan had become extremely picky about the open stylist position in his salon. Conducting interview after interview after the salon closed, Jonathan was practically never around. It wasn't that Kevin minded, but within the past month he saw him less and less. With one stylist down, it meant that Jonathan, Monica and Lori needed to pick up the slack and take on new clients. Being a supportive partner, he knew it was super stressful to take on new clients and have to delegate different tasks. Even though Kevin had begrudgingly offered to come in between his own projects he was managing. Jonathan told him it wasn't necessary, which Kevin found himself feeling very grateful for. He loved spending time with him, but he just didn't want to mix business with pleasure.

Lifting himself out of the bed, Kevin could smell the awful stench of his own odor as he raised his arms and almost gagged. He needed that shower desperately but also needed to go see his sister.

The clanging of metal tools being thrown on top of each other, and the sound of a male's grunt coming from the garage were the familiar sounds of his brother-in-law working on a car. As Kevin walked up the driveway and saw his father's black 1978 Z28 Camaro in Grace and Jim's double garage with Jim bent over and almost halfway into the engine block. Titling his head to the side, Kevin stood there admiring Jim's ass and thought just how lucky his sister was.

"I'm gonna tell Grace on you! Stop staring at my ass!" Jim yelled, looking at Kevin through the crook of his arm. He was still bent over the hood, probably not willing to let go of whatever it was he was doing. Kevin didn't know the first thing about cars, but he was sure Jim had his hands full. Closing the distance he walked up to Jim, who was now straightened up and wiping his hands with a dirty rag.

"Go ahead and tell on me. I am not going to stop thinking my sister is the luckiest lady on the planet now that the two of you are finally together." Kevin said, looking around the garage and noticing Jim's phone with a weird looking type game on it open on the screen. He didn't know that Jim played games on his phone. He really wasn't the type. Puzzles or word searches yes, but not games on the phone.

"Yeah, well I think I'm the lucky one." Jim smiled, grabbing his phone. He shot a look to Kevin that reminded him of when he would catch Calvin or Colin with something they weren't supposed to have. As if his hand was being caught in the cookie jar. Kevin had seen an app like this before; he just couldn't place it.

"Well Mr. Lucky, where is my sister? Is she in her office?" Kevin asked, opening the gate to the backyard.

"Uh, yes, but I wouldn't go there just yet. Maybe come back in like thirty minutes." Jim said, touching the screen of his phone with a slightly wicked grin. Narrowing his eyes to Jim, Kevin turned, craning his neck to see what Jim exactly was doing with his phone.

"What are you doing? Why can't I see Grace?" Kevin huffed. He needed to see his sister and talk about his dream to someone, and considering its vivid nature of intimacy in it, he only felt comfortable talking to her about it.

"You can, just come back later." Jim squinted against the sunlight as he walked out of the garage and he touched the screen again.

A loud agitated cry of "Oh come on!" in Grace's voice came ringing through the air, muffled only because she was inside her writing shed. Kevin looked at the blush across Jim's cheeks and the naughty grin and instantly remembered where he had seen that game before. It was on an app that controls Bluetooth vibrators. And then it dawned on him… Jim was playing with Grace without even being near her and he just told his brother-in-law to come back before he was probably, no, most likely going to have sex with her.

Kevin screwed up his face in horror. He had done some sick crap, but this was the middle of the morning and these two were acting worse than teenagers.

"OH MY GOD! Please tell me you are not doing what I think you are doing?" Kevin said, with all the disgust he could muster and Jim just snickered.

"Your sister has been feral lately and even I can't keep up with her some days." Jim said, and the thought made Kevin's stomach churn.

The idea that his sister was a nymphomaniac was making him want to vomit right there. Shaking his head, not wanting to lose the breakfast he had just eaten before going over to visit just spurned on Jim to erupt in laughter.

"You two are sick! The kids are just inside, what if one of them comes out?" Kevin screeched.

"Cal and Katie are at work and Vivian and Colin are playing a video game, so no chance of that happening. Now if you would please come back in thirty minutes, you can talk to your sister then." Jim said, putting his arm around Kevin's shoulder. Shrugging it off, disgusted and swatting at the strong arm that had been around his shoulder just two seconds prior, he screwed up his face and made another huffing sound.

"Fine! But at least make sure she is clothed and clean up the fucking nympho before I get back here." Kevin spat and turned on his heels.

Beyond frustrated, he was sure that he would have been able to get all this off his chest right this second, but now he was left to wait. With nowhere else to turn, he got into his car and rubbed his eyes, taking in another deep breath. He was tired. That dream really had messed with his head and he just wanted to have his life return back to normal. Decidedly, but still somewhat resistant, Kevin would bury his feelings deep down until he could work through this appropriately. Wanting to just do anything else, Kevin instead would surprise Jonathan with an early lunch.

Sending in his order to Iorio's Deli, Kevin knew that Maria would make sure that the wrap would be made to Jonathan's specifications. His nerves were raw just thinking about broaching the subject with Jonathan after what happened. For some reason there seemed to be an animosity between George and Jonathan. Kevin wasn't sure exactly why, but ever since he and Jonathan had gotten together George seemed to be very distant. All George said was that his gut told him not to trust Jonathan because of the love bombing that he did at the beginning of their rekindling. But what was Kevin supposed to do? Kevin's feelings for Jonathan ran somewhat deep.

Living in a small town wasn't easy, and most of the gay men that lived in the area were either looking for a hook up or were already in a committed relationship with someone. Sure, he could go to the city or any one of the few gay clubs in the area, but again all he had found were really young guys just wanting to have a one-night stand or a non-committed relationship. Kevin watched as so many of his friends and family found the ones that would love them forever and that was all he ever hoped for. Jonathan never talked about the future, which pulled at Kevin's heart, but it was the only real relationship he had ever been in. *One day he would want to be forever I know it,* Kevin thought. He wasn't sure if it was delusion or if it was just wishful thinking, but life could change. People could change.

Pulling up to the deli, Kevin sighed and hoped that for just one day of his life things would go well. No drama, no stress – just peace and harmony. As the familiar door chime went off as he entered, Kevin took his glasses off and looked up. His heart slammed in his chest and he froze. *You have got to be kidding me!* Kevin was face to face with Brendan Moser, again. Brendan's pathetic look wiped clean off his face as his features turned to a wicked sneer.

"Well, well. Look who isn't here with his bodyguard? How's it going, princess?" he asked with utter disdain in his tone. Kevin's heart raced but he was not about to take this anymore. Somewhere in the deep recesses of his heart Kevin summoned courage he didn't even realize he had.

"First off, I don't need a bodyguard. And second I'm no princess. I'm a queen. Get that straight. Now if you will excuse me, I have shit to do, and talking to a steaming pile of one isn't on my list of things to do today." Kevin said, brushing past Brendan as he stood there gob-smacked at Kevin's courage.

"Do you really think that little stunt fooled me last night? I know George isn't your boyfriend. You just got lucky that he will always be around to protect you. But where is he now?" Brendan smirked, but Kevin was not going to take this anymore. He was a grown adult, successful and in a relationship, his life was significantly better than the pathetic man in front of him. His lips turned upright in a smug smile.

"Well, when he left me in bed this morning it was to go to work. So somewhere in town, he making sure assholes aren't disturbing the peace. Sadly, he isn't here to take one in." Kevin retorted, as his smile grew wider with the level of his bravery. *That's right, I'm not that tiny teenager anymore.* Hearing a tiny snicker from behind the counter, Maria gave a knowing wink to Kevin and his heart seemed to slow from the current pounding in his chest. Brendan whipped his head towards Maria, who just smiled back at him.

"Kevin, your order is ready. Give George a big kiss for me when he comes home tonight." Maria said, placing the order into the bag and handing it over to him. His cheeks were hurting so much from the grin on his face. He didn't need Maria's help, but in this moment he was so happy to have so many wonderful friends.

"Thanks love, I will. Give Al a smooch for me." Kevin winked and tried his best not to laugh directly into Brendan's face. Huffing and turning on his heels, Brendan stormed out the door. It was the second time in two days that he had not gotten the best of Kevin and deep inside his heart roared with triumph.

CHAPTER THREE

Grace

Wait, why didn't you tell me Kevin had stopped by before?" Grace asked, as she adjusted her skirt and grabbed her panties from the floor while Jim caught his breath. Tilting his head looking at the app-controlled vibrator that lay on the carpet of her office floor and then back to his hand that was holding a tissue filled with the condom he was just wearing, Grace blushed as Jim arched his eyebrow at her.

"Because you were a bit preoccupied and I didn't think you would want to be sitting there having a conversation with your brother while I tortured you with the vibrator buzzing away inside you." Jim said, reaching over for another tissue to clean himself up before tossing it into her waste basket next to her desk. Her perimenopause had really kicked into high gear. If it wasn't the hot flashes, or the night sweats, it was the increased libido that turned her into a raging lust filled insane woman.

Walking into the tiny half bath that they built onto the shed, she looked at herself in the mirror. Trying to fix the curls Jim had yanked free from her messy bun mid-session and staring at the hickey now blooming on her neck, Grace knew if Kevin came back he was sure to make fun of her... if he wasn't already grossed out at the idea that she thoroughly enjoyed Jim as an afternoon snack.

"He doesn't know I was -" Grace started and looked at Jim's cheeky grin in the reflection of the mirror as he sat on the loveseat pulling up his pants. "Oh my God, you told him?" she screeched, whirling around with her eyes popping out of her head. Gathering himself and the tiny blanket he placed on the loveseat before their afternoon delight, he walked over, bent down and kissed the top of her head.

"My love, you are not a quiet woman. He heard you when you yelled for me to not stop with the app." Jim said, gently moving Grace out of the way to wash his hands. Screwing up her face, Grace knew the exact moment that was and all the embarrassment in her soul flooded her body.

"Oh, come on!" Grace said, as she sat down in her desk chair.

"Oh, for fuck sake, you are still not done? I gave you an extra half hour!" Kevin's voice muffled on the other side of the door. Jim laughed and Grace could do nothing but blush as she reached down and picked up the vibrator off the floor, tossing it into one of the drawers of her desk knowing she would need to clean that later. With a quick kiss on the top of her head, Jim opened the door and there stood an incredibly annoyed Kevin. "You know you're nasty right? In the middle of the day?" Kevin said while holding his nose. "It smells like sex in here, can we go somewhere else to talk or at least open the windows?"

"I will open the windows. So, what did you want to talk about, Mr. Smoochie-face." Grace asked. She hadn't needed Jim to tell her anything, she already knew. Never one to miss out on human interactions, she knew the moment George kissed Kevin that his brain would instantly spiral. Hesitantly sitting down on the loveseat, he let out a sigh.

"I had a dream last night." Kevin confessed, his expression sour. Grace and Jim shot each other looks and then back to Kevin. *After all these years, that crush didn't seem to be gone*, Grace thought.

"Okay. So, you had a dream. Do you want it to be real or are these just feelings you will bury? Because burying your feelings for someone worked really well for two certain people, right?" It hadn't been just Grace and Jim; it was Denise and Hank as well. Grace wasn't going to coddle Kevin on this, especially since he was already back with Jonathan.

"I, I don't know. A part of me just thinks that all these feelings came back up because of Brendan." Kevin explained, which she completely understood. Facing his bully all these years later again to have the one who saved you in the first place still stepping in made sense for all of this to come back up.

"But?" Grace asked. She knew there was more. Kevin sighed, running his fingers through his dark wavy hair and he seemed to focus on one part of the floor not willing to look up at them.

"A tiny part of me hopes." Kevin whispered. Grace's heart sank a little for her brother. It had taken him a year to get over that crush and the tears shed broke her heart back then. Exchanging concerned glances with Jim, Grace moved to sit next to Kevin and wrapped her arm around him and rested her head on his shoulder.

"Listen. I want the world for you, you know that." Grace took his hand into hers and squeezed. "And you know that I will fight for you in any way that I can. But I can't tell you what to do. You are up against not knowing how George feels or if he even likes men. Plus, you just got back together with Jonathan. I thought you were happy?" Grace asked. She knew that although they were back together and Kevin was thrilled, he still harbored a little bit of anger that they had even broken up in the first place.

"I think I am." Kevin said, sounding more like a question than a statement.

"That doesn't sound very convincing. Why don't you just let things settle down, get back into a normal routine again. I feel like with all the new changes and excitement over the engagement that maybe it is just playing on your emotions." Jim cajoled, as he balled up the blanket still in his hand. "I'm gonna head into the house and get lunch going for the kids, but Kev, you know if you need me to do some digging to see where George stands on things I will." Taking a step back into the office, he bent down and kissed the top of Grace's head and left the two to sit.

As they sat there in comfortable silence, Grace's brain was firing on all cylinders. *What if George did have feelings for Kevin? What if living with him had changed his point of view? But damn if Jim was right, and maybe everything just needed to settle down and go back to normal?* Too many variables were in these questions and now she was completely invested to find out what the answers were.

"Okay listen, I need to write, and I know you have work. So just take deep breaths and go get a coffee. Unless… you still need to keep talking then maybe go see Mommy." Grace said, knowing full well that that was the last place he would want to go knowing that Janie would launch into a whole fussing fit. Furiously shaking his head, Kevin got up from his seat and walked over to the door.

"Absolutely not! Gabby Gertie over there will be impossible if I tell her this, and don't be telling Nikki either! I don't need either one of them trying to play match maker over there."

"My lips are sealed!" Grace confirmed she wasn't about to get on his bad side. It was sweet though, that after all these years he trusted her to talk about this. But never one to let the conversation end on just a sweet note, she threw in one last comment. "Around Jim's dick."

Kevin turned, appalled at her comment and shivered at the idea of what she was insinuating. "Eew-wah! Nasty! I don't know who you are but, turn back into my sweet sister. You feral whore!"

"I'm nasty? You're the one who takes it up the ass! Go to work, bitch!" Grace laughed.

"Slut!" Kevin yelled from the gate and Grace couldn't help but smile.

"Love you!" Grace yelled back giggling to herself as she heard a distant *I love you* from Kevin as he walked down the driveway. Normalcy. Kevin's whole world was being turned upside down in just one night and sending him into a spiral. If this continued there was bound to be heartache. And as someone who knew all too well what that felt like, she didn't want to see this for him. Throwing herself back into her desk chair, Grace closed her eyes and prayed that Kevin could move on from this, because deep loves buried deep in your heart would only lead to years of pain especially if you don't know how the other person feels. But what if…what if this was a reciprocated feeling between George and Kevin? It was a pretty good mystery, and she was determined to find out.

The smell of the brown sugar latte swirled in the air as Grace waited very patiently for her drink. *Penstock* was busy, as always, and normally she would go when it wasn't. But it was time for her mid-afternoon brain break and since she had gotten absolutely zero writing done after she talked to Kevin, a stop for her latte seemed perfect. Knowing the pain of having feelings for someone other than your partner was something she was all too familiar with. She loved Jim way before Hank and never stopped. It wasn't fair to Hank, but when Jim moved on - what was there left for her to do? The smartest and most mature thing Jim and Grace should have done was talk to one another instead of acting the way they did. But that was their teenage life, playing stupid games and winning stupid prizes.

Yet, Kevin was an adult. Grace understood that he didn't want to ruin the friendship and relationship he has with George. This was a very dear friend for years, but then she remembered that date night last year. Something on George's face when Denise previously asked Kevin and George to share her that seemed off. Originally, Grace thought it was about being monogamous, but now something in brain went in another direction. Kevin had called George "sexy" causing him to blush. No completely straight guy would do that, right? Jim never blushed when Kevin called him '*hot dick on a stick*' and Mike would just laugh at '*love muscle*'. So why would a cute nickname make George react that way?

A tap on her shoulder stirred her from her rambling brain and she turned to find the exact person she was thinking about.

"Deep in book plotting or not enough sleep?" George asked, pointing to the latte waiting for her on the counter. Grabbing it and flashing him a wink, Grace's devious little brain had an idea.

"Thanks, Big Sexy!" Grace said, waiting for a blush from George, but all she got was a snicker and a smile. *Hm, interesting,* she thought.

"Great, now I got two Cartinos calling me sexy. Guess I gotta watch out, someone is bound to believe it." George laughed as he nodded over to the barista for his order. "Speaking of Cartinos, have you talked to Kev today? He slept through his alarm and was acting all weird this morning. I just want to make sure he is okay." His concern was truly genuine, and there was that tiny twist in Grace's heart. Was this just friendly or more?

"Yeah he stopped by. He came to check and see how the writing was going and had brought lunch over to Jonathan at the salon." Grace sipped, watching for any sort of reaction from George and she wasn't disappointed. George's nose made a slight twitch at Jonathan's name and it was clear that he had his reservations about him. Taking a sip of his own coffee, he turned and started walking towards the door, and Grace couldn't help but follow because this conversation was far from over.

"Well, I just hope Jonathan appreciates your brother. Kev is too good to have his heart broken again. If you want my personal opinion, not that you are asking for it." George looked down at her and Grace arched her brow, very interested in what his take on Jonathan was. "I don't trust him as far as I can throw him." As he approached the cruiser, he put down his cup on the hood of the vehicle and turned to Grace.

"Well, don't sugar coat it on my account." Grace knew he was an excellent judge of character, always has been. She remembered back in high school how he would always let her know what he thought of the guys she previously dated or who were interested in her, and a number of them she had been very thankful for as those young men were only interested in being physical and not actually interested in her.

"I know he is your brother and you want to see him happy, but Jonathan is not the right person for him." Taking another sip of his coffee, Grace saw the tension in his jaw as he said Jonathan's name.

"You are right, I do want to see him happy. So, if not Jonathan, then who? We live in such a tiny town – and it's not like we are busting at the seams with gay men. Hell, even the bisexual men are taken." Grace added, her eyes never leaving his face. She waited, and there it was… a slight blush on his dark-skinned cheeks and a quick change in his breathing pattern when she mentioned bisexual men. Her dad was right. She should have been a poker player or an attorney because she could read people really well.

"Yeah." Was all he got out before taking another sip. He may have been a good detective and great at interrogation, but it appeared there was a tiny part of his heart sitting right there on his sleeve. Grace was gonna let him think about this for a minute, as her gut tingled.

"So, what kind of person do you see for Kevin? You live with him. You've gotten to really know him over the past year. Who should he be with?" Grace's question was fair in her mind. If George only wanted the best for Kevin and wanted him to be with the right person, then he must have someone in mind. George looked around and just shook his head.

"I don't know. Just not Jonathan." George said adamantly. His tone was a step beyond stern and to Grace it was almost as if he had another reason.

"Why? Is something going on that I don't know about?" Now Grace was worried.

"No. Well, I don't know. I don't want you worrying about this before I have all the details. I just have this -" George paused, but Grace was already filling in the blanks.

"Gut feeling? You too? I thought it was just me." Taking another sip of her coffee, Grace saw the tension in George's shoulders decrease the moment she said something. He wasn't alone in worrying that Jonathan would go and do exactly what he did the year before. Everyone was. Janie invited Grace over for coffee and to no big surprise, Judy was over as well. The two older women were just as concerned about Kevin and had spent a better part of her visit going through the list of residents in town that they knew who were gay, bisexual and even pansexual, but with Kevin's aversion to vaginas they stuck with the gays and bisexuals. Grace never face palmed more times in her life than that one singular conversation.

A crisp sharp call on his walkie-talkie came in, breaking the silence. Flashing a smile, George responded and headed into the cruiser.

"We'll figure this out! Let me sleep on it, hopefully I can dream up someone and then we can brainstorm later." George said before getting in and driving off. Grace smirked a half-cocked smile as she walked up the block to her home. *Dream it up pal, hopefully you two idiots will figure it out.*

CHAPTER FOUR

George

The ache in his shoulders had been there all day, since he woke up from his restless night sleep. George spent the night tossing and turned, unable to find just the right spot to sleep. That dream happened again, the one in the crowded bar, elbow to elbow with people, and this time he could smell the beer in the air around him. His eyes were scanning the crowd for someone. He just didn't know who until he felt the body of someone bumping into his back. Only this time, the body was not small and soft. It was taller this time, leaner and when he turned there was a sense of relief when he looked at the person standing in front of him. The faceless person in front of him still said hi, but it was garbled by the sound of the crowd that surrounded them. But whoever they were still had long black hair, shiny almost unreal. The only features on the person's face that he could make out were their lips and their smile. It was warm and inviting, like he had seen them before, touched them. As he moved closer, it didn't feel forced. It was as if he knew them and they knew him and just before kissing them, he woke up.

It was the same way for years, but this time there was a comfort when he saw his mystery person. Like a sense of feeling as if he was home. It was the same feeling he got when he walked through the door after a long shift like today and Kevin had dinner all ready and waiting for him. Living with Kevin became an interesting change in his life. On his own, George made a routine that he enjoyed, but there was a quiet chaos with Kevin, and he found himself enjoying it day after day.

The ankle break didn't just change him physically but also emotionally. Being confined to the couch or his bed for weeks had been torturous. Yet, Kevin made it go by so quickly and it honestly felt like the two of them were living together for years not months. They joked, did puzzles, he listened to Kevin gossiping with Nikki, and watched movies with Denise and Jodi. It had been the first time in his adult life that people were actually wanting to hang out with him, other than the women he previously dated. There had been only three and the last one was Denise.

It was unrealistic, but George had come to the realization that he was holding out for the mystery person his whole life and had yet to find them. As he pulled into the garage, he thought about his earlier conversation with Grace. He really didn't like Jonathan, and after seeing him with someone else at the restaurant the day before, George sat wondering if his hatred for him was making him jump to conclusions. There was no concrete proof. All he saw was two men having dinner in a restaurant and Jonathan wiping another man's mouth clean. Maybe it was a thing, to wipe someone's face clean. Normally he would just let someone know, but maybe it was socially acceptable amongst friends. But he could never recall doing that other than to one of his dates trying to be suave. He definitely couldn't see himself wiping a crumb off of Hank's lips and then putting it in his mouth. But maybe he was the wrong one here, yet his whole body shuddered at the idea of him doing that to Hank, Denise would definitely slap him for that. Shaking his head he needed to just let that image get out of his head.

Reaching over to the passenger seat, he grabbed his work bag and held it tight to his chest, closing his eyes taking two minutes to reflect. Maybe he was just projecting his own self-hatred onto the fact that Kevin had someone and he didn't. If his friend was happy, then who was he to get in the middle of it?

As he opened the door to the condo, the smell of Kevin's specialty hit him square in the face. Closing his eyes, he smiled to himself and put down his bag at the front door. He heard movement in the kitchen and knew Kevin was there. It was great to come home knowing he wouldn't be alone as long as Kevin lived there too. As he turned the corner heading into the kitchen he stopped short at the sight of something he was not prepared to see.

Kevin was lounging against the counter with his head rolled back as Jonathan was kneeling in front of him openly giving him a blowjob right there in the kitchen. Standing there watching Jonathan's head gliding back and forth as Kevin's fingers tangled into his long hair. And despite the fact that he was actively watching an intimate encounter, George couldn't seem to divert his gaze away from Kevin's exposed abs. A year at the gym had done Kevin well. His abs were more chiseled. With all the work he put in, Kevin's torso had developed that cut v in his lower abdomen, something George's hadn't realized as his eyes moved downwards towards Kevin's groin.

A tingling heat warmed his chest and his pulse rushed at the sight of what was happening right in front of him. Shock swirled in his brain, conflicted with the fact that they were doing this right here in his kitchen knowing that he was bound to be home at any moment. Yet, the sight of Jonathan's head moving so smoothly over and over mixed with the tiny gasps and moans coming from Kevin's mouth stirred something deep in George's loins. He shouldn't be looking. He shouldn't feel turned on by this. But he couldn't quite pull himself away. Jonathan moved his hand from Kevin's hip and a small part of Kevin's groin came clear into view as Jonathan reached to massage his balls and Kevin let out a throaty moan as his head rested back onto the cabinet.

George's dick grew hard straining against his pants zipper, twitching at the sound coming from Kevin. He knew then - he needed to get out of there.

Silently, he stepped away from the doorway, not wanting to be seen or heard. It was all too much. Never in his whole life did he ever think he would be seeing Kevin or any man in this sort of situation. Sure, there were pornos of men with women having threesomes, but he had never seen a scene where one man was giving head to another man before, let alone his best friend and roommate. He needed to leave. He needed to get out of the house and away from this sudden desire to keep watching. A part of him wanted to know what they were thinking. Not in the sense of what they were doing and the unfortunate timing, but what it felt like. Did it feel the same as when a woman did it? Were they thinking of each other or just enjoying the sensation?

There had been times when he absolutely was only enjoying the sensation, he wasn't thinking about the person performing the act. In fact, a few times, he would think of someone else just to cross over that orgasm threshold. Doing his best to ignore the building moans coming from the kitchen, he quietly opened the door and headed out shutting the door. without making a sound. With his back to the door, George closed his eyes to take a deep breath in, but all he saw was Kevin's face. His lips parted, his long neck arched back and then the rest of him.

George's body betrayed him as his cock grew harder and he opened his eyes. Blinking, he needed to get away from here as soon as possible.

Mom, I need to get to Mom and Dad's because none of this is making sense.

Standing on the front steps of his parents' home, he needed to get his breathing regulated and back to normal. With the rest of his body now acting a bit normally he thought he was safe. Yett every time he closed his eyes, he saw Kevin. Quickly knocking on the front door, he realized he could have just walked in, however, for some reason, he couldn't move. As the door swung open relief washed over him as his sister, Regina, answered the door.

"Well, shit. It's about damn time your ass showed up. Too busy for your own family to even stop by once and awhile?" Regina snarked looking him up and down. She had an attitude the size of Kentucky, but a heart as big as Texas. And the moment her eyes met his, her whole attitude changed. "Come on, get in. Mommy is feeding the kids."

Walking over the threshold of the house, he immediately felt a wave of relief wash over him. His childhood home was warm and cozy, with deep orange colors throughout, a complete contrast to his very gray palate in his own home. The smell of Mannish Water soup hung in the air, normally a Christmas staple, or whenever someone was feeling down. He knew he came on the right day, at the right time.

"Mama, looks like we have one more for dinner." Regina called from the hallway before they walked in to find his niece, nephew and parents sitting at the dinner table. The sheer delight and glee in his mother's eyes hit George square in the chest as he walked through the doorway.

"Ah, mi pickney! Bwoy where have you been? You told me you would be over last week and you had me fretting over you." Doreen's thick Jamaican accent came through more when she was yelling at him than when she was not. Bending down to hug her, she first hit his arm and then wrapped her arms around his neck, bringing him in for a huge hug. The scuffle of a chair behind him pulled him away, as not two seconds later the towering figure of his father stood at his back.

"You should know better than to make her worry. Me, I understand, but don't be letting your mother fret so much. She only gives me gray hairs because of it." Darius Nicols scolded, then smiled and embraced George. This was better. This was what he needed after what he had just encountered. As Regina set a place next to her, his niece and nephew rushed over for a hug and then scurried off to their seats to finish dinner.

"So, how has work been? No serious crazies that I have to be nervous about coming after you?" Doreen asked as she dipped a torn off piece of her homemade roti into the broth. Even though he was not a kid anymore, he knew there was not a moment when his mother wasn't worried about him.

"No, it's been the usual, so no craziness. Thank heavens." George said, stuffing a fried plantain in his mouth. He knew the line-up of usual questions. Work, women, friends, when are you gonna date again. It was the same every time he was single.

"Ah, good. Have you been out on any dates lately? Or at least anyone of interest?" Doreen asked, causing George to choke a little on the sip he had just swallowed. He knew this line of questioning, it shouldn't have gotten the reaction out of him like it did, but he could still hear echoes of Kevin's moans in his ears. His jaw tensed as he cleared his throat with a sip of water and couldn't seem to look up.

"Nope, no dates." George said, as he lifted his head with his eyes closed, smiling at his mother, and then didn't open them till he looked back down at his soup. *Maybe, this wasn't such a great idea*, he thought to himself.

"Pumpkin, look at me." Doreen said. With a heavy sigh George slowly raised his head and looked at his mother. The gaze of a mother was better than any interrogator on the planet. He knew she was on to him and she wouldn't let it go. George felt lost for the first time in his life, which was beyond out of character for him. It had been little things here and there, but nothing that had made him stop and question things, until today. Slowly rising to her feet, she curled one finger and wiggled it without even saying a word. Looking around the table, all eyes were on him and he knew well enough that if he didn't move quickly she would be calling out his full name.

Pushing his chair back, he followed her out to their sunroom and shut the door behind himself. As she took a seat in her well-worn peacock rattan chair, she patted the chair next to her for him to sit.

"Okay mi bwoy, out with it. Something has you rattled, otherwise you would not just show up unannounced to my home. You always call before you come -" his knee jerked at the word. He knew it wasn't the same, but it still was odd to hear out of his mother's mouth and she noticed. Reaching over to his face, her thumb gently padded over his cheek as if she was wiping away a tear that wasn't there, she gazed into his eyes. "Who?" she whispered.

'Who' was the hardest question he had ever been asked in his life. A single syllable word for him held the weight of the world in it. The dreams of the long-haired woman or person, or whoever in a bar and in his heart he held out hope that one day, he would find them. But what if it had just been that - a dream? An illusion created by a sad lonely man hoping to find his one. His eyes burned and stung as he closed them and he felt the falling of tears he hadn't expected to shed.

"Mama, I don't know what's going on." George whispered as he pressed his cheek into his mother's palm. She got up from her chair and embraced him, a massive man crying in his mother's arms as if he was a child again with a skinned knee.

"Who?" She asked again. He didn't want to say. He didn't want to admit that over the past year Kevin grew on him. Not just in a best friend way, but something more. In the way that he laughed at the stupidest jokes, or that he cried at sappy moments in movies and shows. The way he ate certain foods, or that he seemed to know when George needed his space or would put music on that would completely relax him after a long shift. It was the way he hummed to himself while he was cleaning the dishes and the ridiculous dance he did when he cleaned his room. It was that he had turned George's lonesome condo into a home… their home.

"I can't say -" George paused, "I don't want to say their name."

"Why? Because you think we won't love you? Because we will." His mother's voice was like a song hitting straight to his heart. He knew they would love him and understand. Because this wasn't a sexual thing. That had come on only recently. But to him, their friendship meant a great deal. He would never have defended or been there for Kevin over the years if he didn't love him as his friend. Ever since George went and joined stage crew for the plays back in high school and became friends with Grace, that he took the opportunity to make friends with Kevin. Sure, back then Kevin had a crush on him. Everyone knew, but it didn't stop him from being his friend.

"Because they are with someone else. They are happy and I can't break their heart." George's voice cracked for the first time in years. The weight of the truth and the love in his mother's embrace finally broke that straw that was on his back. Kevin was everything emotionally he ever wanted in another person - his person. But he was with someone else. Jonathan didn't deserve him, but he could at least satisfy Kevin. George didn't even know the first thing about having a sexual relationship with a man and he wasn't even sure he knew how to go about it. He had been with women, but men had the same equipment as him, and although he had touched his own body and taken himself in his own hand for his release, he assumed it would be different.

"Then you, you are a fool." Doreen's tone changed cold. George's tear-stained face looked up to his mother. He couldn't believe she was saying this to him after he came here for some advice.

"I'm the fool?" George flew up from his seat, now towering over his mother. "I'm not the one with a cheater! That man is not right for-".

"Kevin?" Doreen smirked as she arched her brow inquisitively. His heart stopped. How did she know? "Finally, you are on the same page as all of us." She said, sitting back down in her chair. George couldn't believe it.

"What do you mean, finally on the same page as us? Who is us?" George was astounded as he paced the tile floor and ran his hands over his short crew cut, still in utter shock that other people were thinking that he had feelings for Kevin. He did, but that thought stopped him dead in his tracks. He did have feelings for Kevin, and for the first time in his life he was actually admitting it.

"Us. Your family. I'm not one hundred percent sure about Janie and Ken, but I think they have an inkling. Maybe even Grace." Doreen nonchalantly said, as if this was all common knowledge. George stood there remembering the conversation with Grace earlier. Being so adamant about Jonathan not being the right person for Kevin, he even said he would dream up someone who would be perfect for him. He was perfect for him, all except the sex part. That was going to be difficult. But there was something on Grace's face the whole time, she must have been reading him. Shaking his head, trying to rationalize all of this new information, he looked at his mother.

"How am I supposed to do this? I can't march into the house and say, hey break up with him because I have feelings for you. What if he doesn't feel the same? Then I just screwed up my whole friendship." Exasperated at the idea of having to do this, George plopped back down into the chair. Allowing his head to fall back he stared at the ceiling. His brain and heart felt like they were going a mile a minute at the dread of how he was gonna go home, until his phone buzzed in his back pocket.

Pulling it out he prayed it was work, some big fire… anything but who he wasn't prepared to see yet.

MY PERSON

Buzz – Kevin

Hey, not sure what time your shift is over, but I made a pot of Kevin's specialty and put a plate in the microwave for when you get home. I'm heading out for the night; I'll be back tomorrow.

Taking a deep breath in, he just put a thumbs up emoji and tucked his phone back into his pocket. It was now safe to return home, but it wouldn't feel the same. There had been a few times when Kevin would go and spend the night at Jonathan's, usually when George would work overnights, but never on a night when he was home.

"Guess I'm safe for another day. He won't be home tonight." George said. All Doreen could do was nod.

"Is everything alright?" a deep voice from the door asked. George looked up to see his father standing there listening with a smile on his face. George's heart stammered in his chest. He still had to face his father. But if what his mother said was true, that everyone in the family knew then maybe it wouldn't be as bad. George didn't know what to do or say. He felt like he was supposed to explain something, that it was possible that his father would hold some resentment toward his only son for having feelings for another man. Gathering the courage to stand up and expecting the worst from his father, he walked up to him.

"I – I don't know how to say this." George stared at the questioning glance from his father.

"What? That my son has finally found his person? And that it is his best friend?" Darius questioned, his tone calm and even, not what George had been expecting.

"You realize my best friend is Kevin. That means I'm -" George still wasn't sure he could say the word. It wasn't bad. He just wasn't sure what he was supposed to do now.

"Mi son. Yuh a mi pickney, an wi love yuh. Dat a all yuh be to wi, seen? Yuh like woman, yuh still mi son. Yuh like man, yuh still mi son. Love nuh carry no label. Love a love. Dat a it." George's father's true Jamaican coming out for the first time in years since he moved to the states. Darius gathered George into his arms and squeezed and George's large frame broke and the tears started all over again. "Wi love yuh. Nuttin nah go change dat, yuh hear?"

Relief washed over George like a dam being breached and rushing through a valley. He allowed it to crash over him, as wave after wave of love surged around him from his parents. His mother's tiny frame came up from behind him embracing them both, and all he wanted to do was stay there in his parent's embrace as long as he could. Because as his father said, *love is love* and they would never judge him for who he had finally given his heart to.

It was hours later and the darkness in George's condo reminded him of a tomb. There was no music, no sounds of laughter. Even the smell of Kevin's cooking had dissipated as he walked through the living room to the kitchen to find that Kevin left the window open, ensuring the scent of the cooked shrimp would not leave a lingering odor. Closing the window, George went to the microwave and opened it to find the plate Kevin had left him. Now cold and inedible. Tossing it in the garbage, George sighed and brought the plate over to the sink and stopped for just a second. The vision of Kevin and Jonathan from earlier once again coming into his mind. Instead of it stirring up a heat in him, his heart now hurt. His person with another man broke a piece of him. How was he supposed to go on acting like his feelings for his best friend didn't matter? How was he supposed to co-exist with him in such a tiny space and pretend that every time he talked about Jonathan or spent time with him it didn't hurt?

Rinsing the plate and then putting it into the dishwasher, George wondered how he was going to pursue this without making it seem so incredibly obvious. The realization that he was bisexual was not something he was going to be shouting from the rooftops. Yet when he thought about it, there were only a handful of times he had been turned on by men. And in truth it had only been things that had happened with Kevin. He didn't find other men attractive. Just Kevin. And that wasn't what mattered to him. It was the individual that he cared so deeply about.

George realized that at some point the physical aspect of things would come into play, but he wasn't sure how he was going to handle it. Yes, there was attraction. Kevin's lips had been much softer than he originally thought. His body, although masculine, was warm against his and if Brendan had not been there carrying on like an idiotic bigot, who knows what would have happened. However, if Brendan had not been there, George never would have kissed him. Never would have known what Kevin felt like, tasted like. The echoes of Kevin's moans, his long form lounging against the counter and the memory of the feel of him stirred a heat in George's body he had been fighting for too long.

Something primal and beast-like pounded in his chest, and he knew that he needed to separate Jonathan and Kevin. George knew just from the look on Jonathan's face the other day at the restaurant what was happening between his and the other young man was not innocent. Too many times, of Jonathan cancelling plans or blowing Kevin off gave George the indication that he was cheating on him. Even Hank believed that Jonathan was cheating.

While in the gym with Hank weeks ago planning the proposal George hit the weight bench. Kevin had opted to take a spinning class, leaving the two of them to spot each other. Kevin had said that he needed to ride out his feelings and Hank shot George a knowing look.

"Alright Mr. Detective, you gonna to tell me you aren't thinking the same thing as I am?" Hank asked, as he stood over George spotting his 250-pound lift as he laid on the bench. Lifting it up to the rack and resting it, George shook his head and sat up, grabbing the towel and wiping the sweat off his brow.

"What? That Jonathan is cheating on Kevin? That? Or that we are all sick of seeing him hurt over and over again by someone who is just using him?" George took a sip of his water, but it didn't stop the bitter taste in his mouth any time he thought about the whole situation.

"I could say something." Hank wiped down the bar and then went to remove the two twenty-five-pound weights George added, smacking George to get up from the bench. It was an idea. Hank would be the one person to say something about being a cheater, he had done it. Hank wasn't proud of that fact, but he knew what the signs were.

"You? I'm not sure that would go over so well." George knew that Kevin wasn't a massive fan of Hank's, so if he went up to him and told him that he thought Jonathan was cheating on him, it might just throw him into Jonathan's arms even more. "What about Grace? Has she said anything?" George asked as he helped Hank with the weight.

"No, but it doesn't mean that mind of hers isn't running a million miles a minute. She said that the only reason she never divorced me sooner was because she didn't have any evidence. Now if you had proof,

that might be a different story." Hank said through the bench press. George grabbed the weights and put it up on the rack.

"I'm not going to spy on Jonathan just to prove if I am right. Now if I thought he was stealing something, then it would make sense, but he's not. He's just not the right person for Kevin." George said, watching Kevin through the window to the spin class. He seemed to be putting in more of an effort than he normally did and George wondered what was his motivation. When they arrived, Kevin was still down because Jonathan had been a no show for dinner, claiming that a client's process was taking longer than expected. But George knew that wasn't true because he had been on patrol at that time and saw Jonathan lock up the salon.

George didn't know about the date until that morning and was not about to add fuel to the already raging fire that was Kevin's hurt feelings. Since they started going to the gym with George, Kevin would use anger or hurt feelings as his motivation. But back in March when they reconciled, the anger and hurt feelings appeared to have dissipated. Now he went to maintain his weight loss and he had been doing really well, except when something like this would happen. Then he would just get on a bike and ride. Which George thought was a good thing, working out the frustration, but burying the feelings was not healthy. He understood that a little.

"Well, you let me know when you think of someone else he can date. Kev's a good guy. He deserves someone who cares about him the way you do." Hank said through the last rep. George's heart fluttered for a second as his eyes connected with Kevin's, who finally finished his session and was on his way over to them. "Hey, could use a little help." Hank said struggling to get the weighted bar up on the rack above him. George shook his head focusing back on Hank who looked up at him with a discerning eye. George knew then something was off with him. He just couldn't put his finger on it.

Kevin did deserve someone like George and vice versa. There were moments throughout his life when he had questioned why he never connected with someone that made him happy. Out of all of his friends, Kevin was always there, taking him out for a burger and beers just to talk it through. Always building him up, telling him all the wonderful things that he saw in George that he couldn't in himself. Initially, he thought it was just Kevin blowing smoke up his ass, but there was something in his eyes when Kevin looked at George that made him feel better. Like Kevin saw him for who he was. Then a thought crossed George's mind. *Had Kevin been in love with him beyond the teenage crush? Is it possible he missed his chance, all because he denied his feelings?*

He needed to clear his mind, and after the day he had the only thing he could think to do was take a shower and go to bed. Grabbing a pair of lounge pants, tank top and boxers out of his drawers and his towel from the back of his door, he turned the light on in the bathroom and set up his stuff on the shelves. The only room left to remodel was the bathroom. Still with the original 1960's metal shower doors, boring and standard. Kevin had been complaining about how boring it was. He had mentioned that he was willing to pay for a remodel, but with him back with Jonathan talk of the remodel had taken a backseat. Sighing, George slid the mirrored door over to start the water. His eyes looking over the old sad looking tiles when he noticed that Kevin hadn't taken his shampoo and soap with him. But considering what Jonathan did for a living, he would probably have all the toiletries he needed.

Making sure the water was the right temperature, George got in and stood under the water allowing it to cascade over his muscular form. Absentmindedly, he grabbed a bar of soap, not realizing it was Kevin's until he held it in his hand. It was a homemade soap of lavender and rosemary that Kevin had insisted on buying at the Farmer's Market here in town. He didn't care for it, he liked more woodsy smokey tones and this was not that. It was light and floral, but not in a feminine sort of way, he smiled to himself and thought it was just very Kevin.

George had a routine in the shower. He started with his right hand, up that arm, down the right side of his body, then the inside of his right leg, groin, down the left leg, then back up it washing the whole left side, his chest, then down his left arm, his back and then he was done. It took no more than two minutes in total to wash everything except his head. This had been his routine since he was in the Marines, but today he didn't want to leave the comfort of the water or the scent of the soap.

Lathering up his African net scrub, he decided to change his routine. His whole world was upside down, so why not try something new, he thought. Starting at his ankle he ran the mesh up his leg, the roughness from it was comforting as if he was scrubbing away years of denial. And then for a quiet moment he thought of Kevin's hands. They were soft, not rough like the mesh or even his own. Kevin was not one to work with his hands, so they had never been calloused. Wondering if a softer washcloth would feel more like Kevin's hands, a tiny part of him wanted to know. Opening the glass shower door, he saw the washcloth hanging up with the other towels on the rack and hesitated for a brief moment.

What was he doing? He was contemplating using a washcloth just to fantasize what Kevin felt like on his skin while he showered. George couldn't do it. He needed sleep, he had to finish showering and hide in his bed. Coming to his senses, he finished his shower and focused only on his nighttime routine. That was George - routines and rules. It wasn't that he wanted to be predictable. It was just that following the rules and staying in his lane was comforting to him. But now all these feelings, all the realizations did nothing but throw his life into utter upheaval. Just like last year, when he was running and then saw Kevin alongside of him on the track. He had lost his footing and broke his ankle then. Only now, it would be his feelings. No broken ankle to sustain, only the possibility of it being a broken heart he would get instead.

He needed a plan, if he was going to show Kevin that Jonathan was not the right person for him. George needed some kind of proof. He was gonna need help, and he had an idea where to start.

CHAPTER FIVE

Nikki

Placing the frozen package of ground beef on the counter, Nikki realized she had only drunk one cup of coffee and at nine a.m. she should have been on her third. Her night sweats seemed to be getting significantly worse. Last night she had made Mike get out of bed just to change the sheets and then showered before climbing back into bed with only a pair of panties and tank top on. She would have gone to bed completely naked if it weren't for the kids, but Mike told her that she couldn't just lie in bed naked knowing that Mandy still liked to waltz into their room whenever she pleased just to say good morning.

Feeling a wave of heat rush through her body, Nikki went back over to the refrigerator and opened the door, allowing the thirty-five degrees coolness to wash over her. *Perimenopause is bullshit*, she thought to herself. As the fridge dinged its warning bell that the doors had been open for too long, Nikki screwed up her face, grabbed the creamer and shut the doors.

Coffee, she needed more coffee. Grabbing the insulated mug Denise gave her last Christmas, she couldn't help but laugh at it every time she looked at it. The black coffee mug with a tiny devil mug on it and the writing on the cup said *I love my coffee black... like my women and my soul.* Waiting for it to finish brewing, her mindless staring was interrupted by the sound of the doorbell.

Making her way to the front door, Nikki didn't understand why Denise or Grace just didn't walk right in. It was an unspoken rule that her door was always open and you could walk right in. That was until she was looking up at George standing on her front step.

"Uh, hi. What are you doing here? Mike is at a game." Nikki questioned, honestly not sure why George would be standing on her front step. The sheepish gaze he was giving her tugged at her heart, in their entire friendship he never look this way before. With bags under his eyes, he looked like he hadn't slept in days. Motioning to come in, Nikki was now intrigued.

"I actually came to talk to you, if that's okay? I wasn't a hundred percent sure who to talk to about this." George confessed, letting out a sigh he seemed to be holding in.

"Yeah, want a cup of coffee? You look like you could use one." Nikki motioned her head towards the kitchen and George followed, almost like a lost puppy. This was not the strong, confident man she was used to hanging out with. As they entered the kitchen he looked around and saw the mug and gave a slight snicker.

"Denise?" George asked as he took a seat at the kitchen table.

"Yup. She's not wrong though, except for the coffee. I like those light and sweet." Nikki smiled, putting another mug under the Keurig and pressing the start button. George's head tilted to the side, unsure of what he heard.

"Nikki, I've known you forever, how did -" George started saying before they heard the front door slam open and Denise called out.

"Alright Bitch, I need coffee stat and Grace said she needed to talk to us about Kev -" Denise stopped short, not finishing her sentence. "Oh, well hello there Big Sexy! I wasn't aware you were added to this week's meeting of the minds." Denise said, gliding through the kitchen door frame. Nikki knew that things were about to get very interesting now that Denise and Grace were here.

"Who's here? I thought Mike was coaching? I didn't want – OH! George, what are you doing here?" Grace asked.

Grace had called Nikki earlier and thought it was best that she talked to her and Denise together about the interactions between both Kevin and George the day before. Something was up with the two of them. They all felt it after that kiss at the Sun. Normally, Nikki would have talked to Kevin about it, but because he appeared so shocked she hadn't wanted to talk to him just yet, figuring it would only make things too confusing for him.

Handing George his coffee and creamer, Nikki took a seat across from George and she could see the apprehension etched in his face. His hand barely on the cup, his brow furrowed, she knew he was debating even being there.

"Listen, I'm sorry. I don't want to interrupt your coffee session. I -" George started getting up from his seat until Denise put her hand on his shoulder and gently pushed him back down into it. His head lowered, his gaze never leaving the cup and every part of Nikki tingled with the idea that this may be not just about that kiss, but something more.

"Sit your ass down, you aren't going anywhere. Now I know why the three of us came here to chat about. But why are you here?" Denise asked as she made herself a cup of coffee. As Grace took the seat next to George, Nikki glanced over to Grace who bit her lip and smiled back. This was definitely about more than just the kiss, and Nikki couldn't wait to hear about it. She felt honored that George had come to her house. Normally she would have expected George to have gone to Denise or even Grace, especially how close he was with them. But the fact that he came here meant a lot.

"Kevin." George said. As Denise sat down, Nikki couldn't help but look at her and then Grace. She knew it!

"What about Kevin? Is he okay?" Denise asked. George sighed and Nikki was trying extremely hard not to reach across the table and just scream *spit it out already*.

"I think Jonathan is cheating on him. I don't have proof of it other than what I saw the other night, but something tells me Jonathan is still seeing other men." George said. "I came over here to see if Nikki might know something or heard anything."

All three women collectively slumped back in their seats. Sitting there disappointed, Nikki was sure George was finally going to confess his feelings, but instead just dropped a different bomb. Silently exchanging more glances with Grace, there was a part of Nikki that just wanted to shake him. But with George, she was going to have to play the long game.

"I haven't heard or seen anything, but I'm sure if he is, he is going to be doing it secretly considering how close knit this whole town is. If he is going to actively cheat then he is going to do it somewhere else." Nikki reasoned. Kevin hadn't said anything to her about whether or not he suspected anything, and he would have or at least he should have. He would have asked her to find out if someone did indeed see anything knowing the connections in town that she had. But that wasn't the case. Kevin was madly in love with Jonathan and despite all the shady behavior, no one ever told her anything knowing just how close they were.

"Wait. What happened the other night? What did I miss?" Grace asked. Nikki saw the pained expression on her best friend's face at the realization that George had seen something that might be concerning.

"I was on the way to the Sun, after the proposal and I stopped in front of Nico's and saw Jonathan with a younger guy. I figured it was just a friend, but then he went and wiped something off of this guy's lip and then sucked it off his own thumb." George finally looked up from his coffee he hadn't even bothered to drink and caught Nikki's eye. Her gut twisted knowing that was a definite seduction move. Having done that countless times to Mike and him utterly losing what little composure he had, she knew that move all too well and what it signified.

"Fuck off! You have got to be kidding me. He might as well have been blowing him right there in the restaurant." Denise exclaimed and Nikki watched something in George's face change. She couldn't be certain but it almost looked like he was blushing. Tapping Grace's leg under the table, she was hoping she would get the message and wouldn't freak out with what she was going to say.

"Or worse, doing him up the ass right there at the table, all bent over with that weird man bun flopping on the top of his head every time he slammed into him." Nikki said, and George's eyes went right back to the cup and was he now blatantly blushing. Grace audibly made the sound that she was going to regurgitate and then grimaced towards Nikki. Nodding toward George, trying to silently show her his reaction. Finally taking the hint, Grace looked over and noticed, biting her lip. Clearing her throat, Nikki looked at her friends.

"So, without proof we can't break them up. Pretty much everyone wants that, correct?" Nikki paused and everyone bobbed their heads in agreement. "But we have to get Kevin to be the one to leave on his own and be strong about it, not sappy Kevin. We need to give him an incentive to leave."

"What kind of incentive?" Denise asked, flashing a knowing smile.

"Someone else." Grace said, just as George was taking a sip of his coffee and he nearly choked. Nikki tried not to laugh but couldn't help herself. Grace had impeccable timing.

"Someone else?" George questioned in between coughing.

"Ya. Didn't you just tell me you would dream someone up because you wanted Jonathan out of Kevin's life?" Grace asked. Nikki watched a muscle in George's jaw tense and could see the wheels in his head spinning.

"Yeah, I said that but I don't want to -" George started and then stopped. Nikki wanted to scream at him. *Finish the damn sentence, I don't want to be his rebound.* "I don't want to force him into something or into a relationship with someone else just because I don't think Jonathan is right for him." George said. Nikki was now pissed. She couldn't understand why he just couldn't come out and say it.

"Bull shit!" Denise said, and everyone's eyes snapped to her, even George. "You don't want to see him with Jonathan because you want to be with Kevin." Denise said, turning to Grace and Nikki shaking her head. "I'm sorry, I can't do this stringing him along waiting for him to open his mouth. He came here to talk to you," pointing to Nikki, "he is pissed about Jonathan, and for the love of God you are actively blushing about us talking about sexual acts. You kissed your best friend to protect him. And that was sweet and everything. But you wouldn't have done that for Hank, or Mike or Jim if it was them. You did it because you are in love with Kevin and when you love someone you will do anything to protect them."

Nikki couldn't believe Denise had just called George out, but then again she shouldn't have been so surprised. Denise was never one to beat around the bush, and poor George just sat there dumbfounded.

"I, I -" George stammered. Nikki watched as Grace reached over and held George's hand. If there was anyone who could coax something out of someone as gently as possible it would be her. Nikki knew herself and Denise well enough that they couldn't do it.

"Hey, George. Look at me." Grace's tone was soft and sweet. George turned, still so in shock that he just sat there looking bewildered by the whole thing. "Take a deep breath. We are not here to judge you. We have all in some way, shape or form been with someone of our own sex so you are in a judgment free zone here. But the fact that you realize that you love Kevin is not something to be ashamed of or something to hide. Unless we are wrong. You do have feelings for Kevin beyond friendship, right?"

God, she is so good, Nikki thought. Grace shouldn't have been a writer. She should have been an interrogator or a prosecutor because she could get a confession out of anyone. George just nodded his head and took another sip of coffee.

"I wasn't expecting to… ya know? It's just been little things. And I still like women, but with Kevin, I just don't know… it's hard to explain? It's like, he's been my friend for ages and I love him as my friend. But over the past year, now that I have been living with him, and being around him there are just tiny things that he does or says that just hit me differently, if that makes sense. I'm not attracted to other guys. I don't see other men and say, '*oh he's hot*' and I don't look at Kevin in that way either, sort of. He makes these tiny sounds, or looks at me or says something and I… I get turned on, I think. It's different when I get turned on by women, like, it's just reactionary, hot chick plus big boobs equals hard dick. But with Kevin -" George paused and a slight smile spread across his lips. "It's different, slow and gradual. Like it's a really good case. All the clues are in other places and I have to go and find them and then piece them all together. It's that anticipation, I question if I have gotten all my clues and then I wait for them all to fall into place and when they do it's great, I feel accomplished. With Kevin, it's been slow and steady like an investigation. You can't rush it. You rush it, you miss something and your case is out the window. The problem is that he is with Jonathan and definitely enjoying himself. I don't want to ruin that just because of how I feel, especially if he is happy."

Nikki couldn't believe this. He wasn't just into him physically; he was hopelessly in love with Kevin. Taking a sip of her coffee, she sat there wondering how she was going to get this to work. How was she going to break up Kevin and Jonathan so that George could be with him? *We have to find proof,* she thought.

"Okay, well that just solidifies it. Operation Gevin is officially on." Grace said with a smile. George crooked his head towards her, not sure what she meant.

"Gevin?" George questioned.

"Yeah, I'm Team Grim, Nikki was Team Mikki, and Denise was Team Dank. So, you're Team Gevin, George and Kevin. First things first, we need to find out whatever we can on Jonathan, we can't move -" Grace explained and started plotting until George held up his hand stopping her immediately.

"Thank you ladies, but I don't want to pressure him." George said, concern etched deep in his brow.

"And I don't want to see my brother stuck in a relationship with someone who doesn't love or care about him when he could be with you. Someone who actually gives a shit and will protect him from assholes like Brendan Moser." Grace remarked.

"Holy shit, wait… Brendan Moser! That's it. If he hadn't been there, and there was no kiss between you and Kevin, would you still feel this way?" Nikki asked, having a hunch on something.

"Yes, but maybe it would have taken a whole lot longer." George confessed.

"Do you know if Kevin is interested, beyond the high school crush thing?" Nikki asked and heard a tiny cough out of Grace. All three sets of eyes were now on her.

"That kiss may actually have him questioning some things. He is my brother and I can't divulge certain conversations, just that perhaps we find certain situations to put the two of you in so that things progress in your favor." Grace explained as she took a sip of her coffee and then smiled that mischievous smile Nikki loved about Grace.

"So why don't I just tell him how I feel?" George asked, it seemed a simple resolution to the whole thing but there were still some things he had to learn.

"Because Kevin will spiral and then feel guilty and it will be terrible. Kevin has to come to these feelings in his own way. He's kinda there he just needs a nudge. Which is why we need proof that Jonathan is cheating. If he is, then we need to figure out a way for him to find out and then be able to put the two of you into scenarios that will make him start to want to leave." Grace seemed to have a plan. It was devious and sneaky, especially because it was her own brother, but if there was anyone who knew and understood Kevin the best it was Grace. As Nikki looked around the table at her friends, something deep in her stirred and it caused her heart to leap a little. George finally found his person, and it was Kevin. And she was going to do everything in her power to see her friends happy, even if it meant that she needed to cause a little bit of mischief.

CHAPTER SIX

Kevin

Every fiber in him didn't want to be there. Kevin did promise his mom that he would stop in and have coffee, but deep inside, there was always an ulterior motive with her. As he walked through the side kitchen door, the smell of warm fresh baked bread made up for the fact that he was going to have to sustain a full grilling on how things were with Jonathan.

"Ah! I was wondering if you were going to blow me off again or if you were gonna show. Good morning, my dear." Janie said as she pulled a container of butter out of the refrigerator, putting it on the island next to the loaf of bread. Whirling around Janie grabbed the pot of freshly brewed coffee and brought it over to the island setting it down next to the three mugs sitting there waiting to be filled.

"Who's the third cup for? Please not Judi." Kevin wasn't mentally prepared for the Dastardly Duo today.

Although he spent a great night with Jonathan, he left his place feeling slightly hollow. Sex had been great, it always was. But he just felt like something with Jonathan remained disjointed between the two of them for some reason. He chalked it up to his own indecisive feelings about the kiss and the dream. When he confessed about the kiss to Jonathan he obviously was annoyed by it. Kevin spent the rest of the evening trying to explain the entire situation and he seemed to let it go, but then something in what Jonathan said to him made him take pause. Claiming in a tyrannical tirade Jonathan argued that George kissed him because he had deep seeded feelings for Kevin and he was taking his chance to break them up by finally kissing him. Kevin knew that wasn't true. George was just trying to protect him, that was all. Yet a tiny flutter in his heart leaped at the idea that it could possibly be true.

"No, Gracie was supposed to come but she texted me that she couldn't make it. Apparently, something came up." Janie said as she cut into the loaf of bread that was still steaming.

"Oh, kids okay?" Kevin asked as he sat down and reached for a slice of bread, smearing butter on it.

"Oh yeah, everyone is alright. Apparently she is over at Nikki's. George stopped by and wanted to talk to the girls about something." Janie nonchalantly mentioned it as if Kevin should have known. He hadn't talked to George since he woke him from that dream. There was a little bit of comfort to him that George didn't come home before leaving to go spend the night with Jonathan. But the truth was, it was more than that comfort; it was utter relief about not running into him again so soon. Shoving the buttered bread into his mouth and tasting it for the first time, he moaned a little as he let the salty sweet flavor rush over his tongue. It was perfect as always.

"Uh sir, I don't need you having an orgasm right there while eating my bread, thank you very much!" Janie scrunched up her face, slightly disgusted by the sounds he was making. Kevin stopped and looked aghast; he didn't realize that he made so much noise as he ate. He could only imagine what other people must think of him when he eats and he wondered if he had done that before or at least if he did, how many times he had done it?

"Sorry, I didn't even realize I was doing that, it's just so good." Kevin mumbled as he shoved another bite into his mouth. Janie just shook her head in dismay.

"You know, I did teach you manners. Perhaps you should use them." Janie scolded, Kevin rolled his eyes knowing that she meant well. Pouring him a cup of coffee and then one for herself, she finally sat down with a tiny 'oof', poured some creamer into her coffee. "So how is work? Any new projects?" Janie asked, always starting off her line of questioning about work. Sighing, Kevin knew she wouldn't understand but he was going to try and explain it anyway. But then her phone buzzed on the counter and she reached for it.

"Work is fine. Nothing new, just maintenance on all the sites. One of them got hacked last week so I had to program a firewall. I wanted to put in a logic bomb, but considering the company I was working with I didn't think it best to use illegal coding. Great to keep people out, but I could literally go to jail and I'm not sure I should do that. So, I created a honeypot instead." Kevin explained and sat watching his mother paying more attention to her phone than what he was saying.

"Mmmm honey. Where did you get it?" Janie said, having not heard an entire word he said. Now visibly annoyed, Kevin huffed to get her attention. If she wanted him to come over for coffee the least she could do was actually listen.

"Okay, I'm leaving. If you are going to pay more attention to the phone than me, I will leave you to it." Kevin barked, getting up from his chair. Janie placed her phone down and pouted her lip up to him.

"I'm sorry, I saw it was Grace and she just mentioned something interesting that is all. I'm sorry. You mentioned hacking, firewall, a bomb, and a honeypot. I caught some things." Janie tried to explain, but now he didn't give a crap about his job he wanted to know what Grace said.

"What, something interesting? Spill it woman." Kevin demanded as he sat back down.

"Maybe you already know. Who is George interested in? Grace said she is helping him out with someone he is interested in." Janie asked, her scrutinizing gaze washing over him. He didn't know. As far as he knew George wasn't seeing anyone or interested and a part of his heart twisted. Kevin was with Jonathan, so why did he suddenly feel like the wind had been knocked out of him? The idea that George was possibly going to be dating was not unheard of. George was the perfect package. He was respectful, responsible, kind, generous and ludicrously handsome. The way he moved was almost cat-like despite his hulking frame. His smile could cause you to forget to breathe and the warmth of his body could melt someone's insides. Kevin felt a rushing heat tingle across his face at the memory of George holding him close just before kissing him… how he pressed him closer and how his dick had twitched the second their lips had met.

Waving her hands in front of him, Kevin hadn't realized that he spaced out and looked up, blinking rapidly back at his mother. Taking a sharp ragged breath in, he focused back on her face and stared back at her.

"Where did you just go? You zoned out when I mentioned George being interested in someone." Janie asked. Her analyzing gaze was something he could read a mile away.

"I was just running through my head who he could be interested in and no one comes to mind." Kevin said, taking a sip of his coffee, praying she believed the lie.

"Liar." Janie spat. *Damn it,* he thought. "Next time don't blush while you are thinking about him. Also, I heard about the kiss. You want to talk about it?"

"I'd rather go back and talk to you about work." Kevin smirked. He knew it was pointless. This was the real reason she wanted him to come over. She must have heard about the kiss and was worried.

"You are turning into your sister." Janie snipped. Well, that caught his attention, he wasn't like Grace at all.

"Excuse me, I am nothing like Grace. I am in a relationship and I am very happy." Kevin pronounced, watching Janie - who had been looking down at her cup - slowly raised her eyes and said, "Are you?"

Was he? His gut lurched. *Was he happy or was he just happy to be in a relationship?* A part of him was happy to be back with Jonathan. But there was a minuscule part of him that always worried. It was his own secret that Kevin knew Jonathan would much rather be in an open relationship - able to be with whoever, however and whenever. His sexual appetite was unmatched and if Kevin was being completely honest with himself, the absolute shock when Jonathan went down on him right there in the kitchen still stunned him. He was sure that George was about to come home any second, luckily for them he hadn't. He would be utterly mortified if he strolled right into that scene. But just because the sex was good, didn't make the relationship a good one.

"I think so. I... I don't know." Kevin confessed in a whisper. His eyes fell to his cup and wondered what it would be like to be in a partnership with someone who you were one hundred percent sure of. Something like his friendship with George. It was solid. There was no chance that George would ever stab him in the back or choose someone else over him to be friends with.

"Why don't you ask Gracie for the keys to the cabin? No one has been up there in a while. Clear your head with fresh mountain air for the weekend. It's quiet, you can see the stars," Janie painted the picture of the perfect mountain retreat but she always seemed to forget the one thing he hated.

"No Wi-Fi! I can't work if I don't have Wi-Fi." Kevin griped.

"You don't need to work on the weekend! You can take two nights and relax for crying out loud. Daddy and I can go up with you if you want." Janie said, refilling her mug with coffee and all Kevin wanted to do was scream. The idea of him and his parents up in the woods for the weekend sounded awful.

"No, that will be alright. I'll see." Kevin said, still completely confused and not sure of anything now. His heart hurt and now so did his head. He knew he should have cancelled on his Mom. He loved her, but now he was even more twisted than he was right after that kiss.

Hours later, he went from intrigued and interested about who captured George's heart to completely pissed. The girls were keeping a secret from him. He wasn't sure who he was pissed at more, Denise, Grace or Nikki? They were his core and they were plotting without him. And that made him furious.

Storming up the driveway, he saw Jim back working on the Camaro with his dad right next to him. His feet hitting the pavement so hard, both Ken and Jim looked up from under the hood as the sound echoed through the garage.

"Hey, what are you doing here?" Jim asked and all Kevin could do was hold up his hand as he unlocked the gate stomping towards Grace's office. "I wouldn't do that if I was you." Jim yelled.

"Well, you're not, so suck it." Kevin yelled over the fence and started pounding on the closed door. "Grace open this fucking door." He demanded.

"Someone better be dead, dying or missing a body part. I am writing." Grace yelled back, but he was not letting up.

"Someone is going to be if you don't open the door. I know about your little meeting." Kevin said. He heard clambering from inside the office and Grace yanked the door open.

"And? So what! I had coffee with the girls and George was there. What's your problem?" Grace snarked, turning on her heels, she sat down in her chair crossing her arms, waiting for his rebuttal.

"Since when is George in your little coffee clutch?" Kevin asked. George was not about to start talking to the girls about stuff. Jim or Hank yes because they went to the gym and ran together, heck even himself, he was his roommate. So why the girls?

"Why are you so pissed? A friend wanted to hang out and have an intellectual conversation with a group of intelligent women. More men should want to do that. Maybe you should do it sometime and not just gossip." Grace was being incredibly impossible and all Kevin wanted to do was smack his own sister for her sass.

"Why was he there, Grace?" Kevin asked. He was dying inside to know. "I will call Nicole this second and she will spill all the tea, so just tell me." Grace raised her eyebrow and smiled.

"Go ahead, there is nothing to tell." Grace said, as she turned, uncrossing her arms and went back to typing. He was going to get it out of her in some way, he just needed to play whatever game she was playing.

"So, he didn't come to you guys to set him up with someone?" Kevin asked, pretty confident that she would lie and he would catch her in it. She kept her eyes on the computer and kept typing.

"He did." Grace confessed, Kevin's heart dropped into his stomach. She hadn't lied, she was calm, cool and collected, - typical Grace.

"And? Who is it?" Kevin needed to sit for this. That stupid kiss screwed up his whole life as he knew it. He was happy in his relationship; George was an amazing roommate and now he was questioning everything and his best friend was keeping a secret. *Fucking Brendan Moser! If he hadn't come back to town then he wouldn't be in this situation!* Kevin thought to himself.

"Laney Callahan." Grace responded and just kept on writing. Kevin sighed out a breath he hadn't realized he was holding. His heart was pounding and he wasn't sure why. Was he expecting Grace to say a different name? Or perhaps was he hoping that it was him? His stomach twisted again at the thought. That tiny shred of hope he tucked away in his heart shattered. He wasn't even sure why he would think it would be him.

"Oh. Um, who is she?" Kevin asked. His words nothing higher than a whisper and Grace just kept typing, not moving or turning towards him.

"She's a mom from the PTO, her husband left her last year. I guess with George working security at the football games, they had met. So, he asked us to see if she would want to go on a date. Guess he is ready to settle down. He can't be the lone wolf forever right?" Grace asked. Time to settle down? It was, he guessed. So much of him always held that tiny hope that Jonathan would get his act together and finally commit to wanting to get married, but every time Kevin would bring it up he would instantly change the subject. Closing his eyes and lowering his head, he took in a ragged breath, trying to keep the tears at bay and just nodded.

"Yeah, well that will be good for him, right? Finally found his person." Kevin wiped the tears that slowly escaped and sniffled before straightening up heading to the door. "Well, good for him." He paused for a moment still unsure if his next words were the right way to go. "Uh, you think I could get the keys for the cabin this weekend? Just wanted to get away for a little if that's alright?" Kevin prayed she would say yes. Bobbing her head, her curls blocked her face as Grace went into her desk drawer and left the keys on the corner of her desk. Without looking at her face, he knew she was crying. Her heart was breaking for him. Grabbing the keys off her desk, he went to the door turning the knob and heard her tearful breath before saying, "I'm sorry."

And he knew she was. This was out of her hands, and there was nothing more that she or anyone else could do about it. He needed to accept that Jonathan was going to be his person and hopefully it would be forever, but he wasn't going to hold his breath.

Walking through the door Kevin threw his keys into the key dish and missed. The clang of the keys hitting the floor echoed through the living room, prompting George to pop his head out of the kitchen. Kevin couldn't show how devastated he was. He needed to be happy for him. George was ready to start dating again and he should be happy.

"Hey." George shyly said, cleaning his hands on a kitchen towel. Kevin's eyes drifted over George, his large frame looked almost brooding with the light from the kitchen illuminating him. It took everything in Kevin not to rush over and beg him not to date Laney. He didn't know her, but he knew George had been his friend forever, his knight in shining armor, and he wasn't sure he was willing to share him with someone else. He wanted to run into his arms and kiss him and say, '*You are my person, no one else*' but he couldn't. He was still with Jonathan and he still had feelings for him as well. The indecisiveness in his made his heart ache, so he buried it.

"Hey," Kevin said. He needed to make it light and pretend like he didn't know. "How was your day?" *A brave face, I will put on a brave face and pretend like nothing happened*, Kevin told himself. George took a step closer and Kevin felt almost pulled to him.

"It was okay. I made some dinner if you're hungry." George said. Kevin could smell the pot roast and it smelt amazing but he didn't have it in him to even want to eat.

"I filled up on bread earlier at Mom's, so I'm stuffed for now." Kevin averted his eyes from George, the more he looked at him, the harder it was to even have a conversation with him.

"Okay well, let me know what you want for dinner tomorrow and I'll -" George started, but Kevin needed to just end this conversation.

"Actually, you don't have to worry about me. I won't be home. I'm gonna take a few days and go to the cabin." Kevin still couldn't believe that he was about to take his mother's advice, but sometimes she was right. The best thing to do was get away from everything and everyone. George took another step closer; concern etched into his face and somewhere in the depths of his brown eyes, sadness reflected back on him.

"Did I say something or do something wrong? You've been acting a bit different since -" George stopped, he didn't need to finish that statement... or maybe he didn't want to. Moving closer, George now stood in front of Kevin, but he still couldn't bring himself to look directly at him again. George reached out to Kevin's arm as he lazily slid it down to his wrist causing tiny ripples throughout his body and goosebumps on his skin. Kevin couldn't even hide it if he wanted to, his own body giving him away. "I'm sorry." George paused. "I know I shouldn't have kissed you, but I thought it was the only way to stop Brendan from messing with you for good. I feel like I broke something, like your trust or -" Kevin snapped his head up to George, whose face was so close yet so far.

"No, God no. I appreciate what you did, it was -" Kevin needed to remember to keep things light. "It was fine. I just want to take some time away, that's all. Big issues with a client this past week and I wanted to get away." Kevin was only half lying.

"To the cabin? When was the last time you went up there and did rustic stuff?" George asked. There was a tiny smile and a glint of menace in his eyes. He was busting his chops like he used to before the stupid kiss. Taking a deep breath in, Kevin finally relaxed. His friend was standing in front of him again and it made the ache in his heart ease.

"I go. Not often, but I do go and I have even camped in a tent before, I will have you know. I was in the boy scouts, I know how to chop wood, start and cook on an open fire. I've even made bread in a cast iron Dutch-oven. Have you, Marine?" Kevin smiled. The change of subject was helping. It felt like he was just talking with his roommate again.

"As a matter of fact, I have. Maybe I will show you some stuff I learned in cold weather training some time. But in the meantime, enjoy the cabin. I would love to have some peace and quiet, I only took today off, but I'm twelve tomorrow and twelve the next day. So, I will be working while you are relaxing." George smiled and turned heading back into the kitchen. "You sure you don't want anything to eat?"

Kevin smiled and shook his head no; he wanted to pack and get as far away as he possibly could. He wanted to ask one last thing, but he was afraid.

"I'm good on the food front. But what about you? Besides work, do you have plans this weekend?" Kevin asked, he was hoping he would say no. Two twelve-hour shifts were hard on him, Kevin had seen it firsthand. George would normally come home, eat, shower and head to bed. But then George's expression changed from being happy that the two of them were having such a good conversation, to suddenly looking like he was a kid caught with his hand in the cookie jar.

"I do." George was being vague, clearly not to let Kevin know what he was doing. Suddenly losing what little appetite he regained, his stomach lurched with that rancid pang again.

"Well, have fun. I'm gonna go pack, I think I may leave a little early. The cabin is only two hours away and I think the rush hour traffic should have died down by now. If I leave soon I may be able to catch the sunset." Kevin said, turning wanting to storm out of the kitchen, but if he did he was bound to have George chase him asking why he was in such a rush to leave. He was the reason, but he wasn't about to let him know. Status quo, he needed to show that all was still the same. No change, except that his heart was messing with his mind.

"Kev," George whispered and Kevin stopped, not willing to show him the tears that were stinging his eyes. "Be safe, text me when you get there." Kevin just nodded and headed into his room, shutting the door and all his pain behind him.

CHAPTER SEVEN

George

His phone started buzzing non-stop with texts from Nikki, Denise, Grace and now Laney since sitting down with them over coffee. Apparently Laney owed Grace a massive favor from years ago promising Grace that when the time came, she would repay her. Grace and Nikki, always with their pulse on the happenings in town did some digging. It turned out that Laney used to get her hair done by Jonathan, but not anymore. George had learned that the one thing you don't do is mess up a woman's hair, whether it was her color, cut or in his sisters' cases their weaves.

Laney swore never to go back to Jonathan after her last visit to the salon because he had spent more time flirting with a new client rather than focus on Laney's hair color. And Jonathan being the narcissist he was, didn't even bother to fix it. He claimed that her hair looked fine and that there weren't any discolored bands, *whatever that was*, in her highlights and that she was just getting too old and the process wasn't taking to her hair the way it used to.

Fortunately, she had found a new stylist and they fixed it making her extremely happy and swearing she would never sit in Jonathan's chair again. That was until Grace called and asked her to go back to Jonathan for another appointment. Promising that she would not make her get a color, Laney called in for a last-minute haircut and George would make a guest appearance. He had spent most of the day before with the girls orchestrating the whole thing, and fortunately, with Laney's bitterness towards Jonathan she was more than happy to destroy him, even if it meant that Kevin might get hurt. But that wasn't the goal. Kevin would only find out the truth and George would be there to help him through it.

It was all so manipulative in his mind, but Nikki, Denise and Grace assured him that the sneakiness and covert mission they were conducting was for the benefit of Kevin. Grace mentioned something about a secret weapon and the less he knew the better.

It was halfway through his shift when he got a text that Laney was now at the salon. Luckily, it was his lunch and he had the football jersey that Mike gave to him to deliver to Laney for her son. Pulling up in front of the salon, he watched through the big bay window as Jonathan flirted with another man - the same one from the other night.

Preparing for a shit show, he grabbed the jersey and headed into the salon. Walking through the door he caught Laney in the reflection and she smiled. Jonathan, however, was completely gob smacked and stepped away from the younger man.

"Uh, what are you doing here?" Jonathan's words dripped with disdain as he screwed up his face, glaring at George like he was a solicitor trying to sell him something.

"Hi, nice to see you too. I'm here for Laney." George said with a smile. That odd little beast in his chest wanted to punch his pretentious face. Jonathan's glowered glances between Laney and George as if they both said they were covered with lice. George turned his head and winked at Laney, whose smile widened.

"Aw babe, thanks for stopping by with the jersey, you could have given it to me on our date tonight." Laney said. George knew if he was going to sell this he would have to bend down and give her a kiss. But he had learned his lesson, no more kisses on the mouths for anyone, except maybe one person. He bent down, placed a tiny kiss on her cheek and placed the jersey in her hand. Righting himself, he said loud enough for everyone in the salon to hear.

"Tonight, for dinner - my place? Kevin is away for a couple of days so we will have the whole place to ourselves." George wasn't sure if Kevin let Jonathan know or not about him going away, but the annoyed gasp behind him gave him a clear indication that he was in the dark.

"Um, did you just say Kevie is out of town? Why didn't he tell me?" Jonathan asked, his hands on his hip and George laughed inside. *So, Kevin didn't tell you, that's interesting.* Shrugging, George turned and gave him his best bewildered look.

"I don't know, but I know there is no Wi-Fi, so I guess you will need to ask him when he gets back on Sunday." George said. Something in Jonathan's expression changed as he exchanged glances with the other stylist standing next to him. George knew that look. Jonathan was going to capitalize on the fact that Kevin was away. His heart slammed in his chest knowing that this man right in front of him was planning on breaking Kevin's heart and didn't care. His blood rushed through his veins so fast he could hear it in his ears, and there was a part of him that felt his vision getting blurred with rage until he heard the dinging of the bells on the salon door. Turning to compose himself, he came face to face with Mrs. Locke and her warm smile.

"Oh hello, is everything okay here?" Mrs. Locke asked as she looked between Jonathan and George. Smiling down at the retired school secretary, he wanted to reach down and give her a hug. He had just seen her the other day when he visited with Nikki.

"Everything is fine. Just running an errand for a friend." George explained, then turned to Laney. "I'll text you about tonight."

George inclined a nod to Jonathan and left. Hoping that the plan would work, all he needed to do was wait. Which would only make the next six hours that much more painful to deal with.

Standing at the high polished marble table bar grabbing his drinks, George thanked his buddy Robby for the recommendations for the mocktails knowing that he had to go to work the next day. According to the intel he received from Nikki, who got it from her source - Jonathan was planning on meeting up with the other male stylist in the shop here. Making sure they got the most remote table, Laney and George sat in the corner of the dimly lit bar with an order of disco fries they were able to order from the diner next door.

"Do you think he will show?" Laney asked in such a hushed tone.

"If the information is correct then yes, otherwise you got yourself a night out with me. I just wish I was better company." George chuckled; Laney smiled warmly to him.

"I gotta say, Kevin doesn't even know what he has. I wish my husband had been as determined as you are. Then I wouldn't have asked for the divorce." Laney said, taking a sip of her drink, frowning slightly. "Uh, I wish we didn't have to be such responsible adults. This needs some booze."

They both laughed. They were at a bar drinking non-alcoholic mixers, which was fine with him, but he understood the idea. With all the pressure he was under to get proof that Jonathan was cheating on Kevin, he could really use a beer or something harder. Figuring he would make use of the situation; he decided to find out a little more about his cohort in crime. Laney was truly lovely. She was an office manager for a fuel company, a sports mom, and her son was involved in not just football but basketball and baseball. Fortunately for her, Laney and her husband did co-parent well together. They may not have dealt with a difficult marriage, but her ex-husband, Louie, was never around – a true work-a-holic.

He understood being a work-a-holic. He was one too. But for Kevin he would make time. He truly enjoyed every second he spent with him. It wasn't a chore or an act. Kevin made him feel complete. That was it. When he was with Kevin, he felt more like himself than any other person in the whole world, and it was completely judgment free and the feeling was mutual. Yes, Kevin had his bad habits and quirks, but Kevin wouldn't be who he was without that.

Sitting there enjoying the light banter and stories that Laney was sharing, George began to wonder if Jonathan was ever going to show. But the very second he thought it would never happen, the door opened and in swept Jonathan and the other stylist from the salon. It was showtime.

As they sat in the only table in the bar that was still open, Jonathan sat down and moved his chair right next to his date. George had the perfect vantage view. Years of stakeouts, he knew just the perfect placed to position himself for surveillance. Situated so that he knew both Laney and he would be shielded but could still survey what was going on. It didn't take long for Jonathan to initiate tiny touches with his *'date'* as they were practically nuzzling each other right there in the open.

Laney scoffed as Jonathan placed a tiny kiss along his date's jaw line and she turned her head in disgust.

"How is Kevin with this guy?" She asked. Everyone was wondering the same thing, but George knew why. Because this was an affair Kevin had no knowledge of. If he did, George knew Kevin would end it. As he took out his phone and silently snapped pictures, his heart sank and pounded in his chest. This wasn't fair to him. He deserved someone who was going to treat him with all the love Kevin held in his own heart. A fierce protective love that would keep Kevin safe for life.

As they watched the two other men at their table practically making out right there in the bar, Laney and George sat in uncomfortable silence. He wanted to rush right up to the table and punch Jonathan in the face. The audacity to go running into the arms of another man the second your boyfriend goes away was despicable. But

George knew he couldn't. So instead, they sat there waiting for the moment they could leave.

"The second that Jonathan gets up and heads to the bathroom we should be able to leave without being noticed." George said. Laney nodded in agreement.

"I'm glad Kevin has someone like you. Even if after all this he is still just your friend, I don't know many people who would go to such lengths to make sure someone is loved." Laney reached out and held George's hand. "My only concern is that if he doesn't see what you want him to, he may pull away. I mean this is kind of sneaky. I just hope he sees what you have been doing is best for him." She said as she stuffed a disco fry in her mouth.

It was sneaky, but Jonathan had been sneakier for ages now, and George was not about to let Kevin be played for a fool anymore. As he scrolled through the pictures he was able to capture, George's blood boiled. He needed Kevin to know this immediately, not days later. Feeling a gentle tap on his arm from Laney, he looked up and saw Jonathan getting up from his seat and heading into the direction of the bathroom. Now was the time to leave. Laying down a tip on the table, George and Laney got up and headed to the front door.

Fortunately, Jonathan's boy toy was facing the opposite way and he hadn't seen them leave. As they walked to the car in silence, George thought about how sweet Laney was being about this whole thing.

Opening the passenger door, Laney just looked at him and shook her head.

"I called an Uber, if you don't mind waiting with me." Laney said with a soft smile. George didn't understand.

"We came together; I can drop you off at home." George retorted. Smiling and shaking her head, she started to laugh.

"God, you men are dense! Listen, you just found out that Kevin's been cheated on by that idiot and you aren't going to rush up there and sweep him off his feet? Morristown is closer to the Poconos than Toselle Park! Just wait with me and then head up there and win your man. I wish I had someone as determined as you to want to date me. A covert mission to unlock the truth, play spies? I'm gonna tell you this was actually fun and Kevin is lucky to have someone who loves him as much as you do." Laney said. Love. He hadn't said the word. Strong feelings for sure, attracted yes, wanted to be with him definitely – but love? He hadn't thought about that. George loved things that Kevin did, but was this love that he was feeling?

"Yeah, um, I hadn't thought about that. Love." George said sheepishly. Laney arched her brow skeptically looking at him.

"Okay, well, as a woman, if someone did something like this for me, I would instantly think they were in love with me. So, that's something to consider when you go rushing up there to blow up his relationship." Laney said, checking her phone to see where her ride was and fortunately they were just pulling up. As she waved down the car, George shut the passenger door.

"So, do I not go? I'm confused. He doesn't need to be cheated on. It's not right, he deserves better." George called after her as she opened the Uber ride's door. Turning to him, she grinned and gave a wink.

"So maybe instead of telling him about the affair, you go up there and just tell him how you feel. And then you can tell him about the affair after he realizes he is making a mistake with Jonathan. If he cares about you and has feelings for you, Jonathan won't matter anymore." Laney spelled it all out. George had to be honest with not just himself, but Kevin. He knew there was something between them – there must be. As he watched the car drive off, he got into his own and took a few minutes to think back on the past year.

He felt lost. He didn't know who he was or what he was doing anymore. All he knew was that since that kiss, something deep inside him awakened. Part of his soul finally felt at peace. Tears of awakening burned in his eyes; he spent his whole life being friends with someone who knew him better than anyone else. Who put up with all his quirks and moods. Who stood by him with countless girlfriends, passed over promotions at work and even nursed him back to health.

And the whole time, his person stood there with him. That primal beast stirred in his chest and he knew just what to do. Because he would be *damned* if he was going to let his person slip through his fingers any longer.

CHAPTER EIGHT

Kevin

The inky black sky was incredible up in the Poconos. The lack of ambient light to drown out the stars made the sky look like a sparkling tapestry. Sitting in front of the fire pit in the oversized Adirondack chair, Kevin wrapped his blanket around himself as the air was much cooler up in the mountains and the breeze off the lake was slightly chilling. As he took a sip of his hot chocolate, he tried not to think of George or anything going on at home, but it was no use.

He played it over again and again in his mind about what to do. There was too much tension lately with George since the kiss, and the only thing he could think to do was to see if Jonathan wanted him to move in. But he knew that was not going to happen. Kevin needed to be real with himself, Jonathan was not looking to share his space with someone. Otherwise, Kevin would already be living with him instead of George.

Resting his head back into the chair, he stared up to the stars. Squinting up to the sky, even though he had put on his glasses, he sat in quiet contemplation. How simple it is to be a single ball of gas millions of miles away combusting in space, shining brightly for the tiny humans to look at. Closing his eyes, he wondered if stars manifested feelings - would they be looking for a partner? And what would happen if that star was possibly in another solar system? Would there be a gravitational pull that guided them to each other? Of course, none of that made sense. It was the rambling of a man completely lost on what to do in his own life that he was creating scenarios for stars.

As the breeze drifted over his face, he smelt the familiar scent of George's cologne in the air. Delusion and hysteria officially kicked in. Kevin knew that George was working and he had no idea where Grace's cabin was. That was until he heard the slight padding of feet on the gravel path to the fire pit.

Opening his eyes and hurling himself out of the chair, he expected to be face to face with an attacker with the same cologne, but instead, there in the night was George. The moonlight bathed his form in a soft gentle glow and he looked almost like a moving statue as he approached.

"Hi." George whispered. Kevin's mind exploded.

"What are you doing here?" Kevin asked, watching George standing perfectly still as if he was glued to the path. They stood there blinking at each other for what felt like hours, yet it was just mere seconds. George swallowed hard before speaking.

"I needed to talk to you." George whispered again. Kevin was pissed, this was his time away from everyone and the one person he needed not to be around had intruded in his space. It was childish and immature, but this was supposed to be his time to figure out what the Hell he was going to do with his life. George being here, tempting him whether he realized it or not was not going to help.

"Why? We live together. You couldn't wait till I got home?" Kevin snipped, hastily unraveling himself out of the blanket, throwing it down onto the chair and heading down to the water leaving George behind.

"No. I needed to talk to you *now*." George said. Because of the distance that Kevin was putting between them, George was now yelling. George never raised his voice so it was odd to hear him at that level.

"Trust me, it can wait. Now will you please leave? You are infringing on my solitude and soul-searching time. Besides, you have work and other plans. You shouldn't have come all this way just to talk to me." Kevin spat. George walked up behind him and kept a foot of distance between them.

"Solitude and soul-searching? Since when? You told me that you were getting away because you had a rough week." George asked. His skepticism dripping from his words only pissed Kevin off further. Kevin's heart began racing at the idea that he wasn't allowed his alone time.

"Since now. Besides, you had *other* plans, didn't you? So go home, I'm busy." Kevin sneered and crossed his arms across his chest. As the crunching of George's feet on the gravel path started to fade away, the tears began to stream down Kevin's cheeks. He had just told George to go home. Yet every fiber in his being wanted him. He wanted him here right beside him. There was no denying it to anyone, let alone himself that he wanted George's strong arms wrapped around him and his lips, those unbearably soft lips on his. George's woodsy cologne still lingered in the air as if he was right behind him.

Kevin was being ridiculous and he knew it, and his heart ached. Not only telling his friend to leave, but the one he really wanted to be with. That he might have just sent him on a path into someone else's arms.

It's not fair! He is MY PERSON, he thought.

If Jonathan was here, he knew in the secret place in his head that he would not have felt so terrible about pushing him away. He didn't want George to walk away; he wanted him here. Whirling around he hit George square in the chest.

"You walked away. I heard you walk away!" Kevin said, and he wasn't sure if his mind was playing tricks on him until he saw George's shoes in his hands.

"I didn't drive all the way up here to be told to leave. There are some things I need you to know and I need you to be calm when I talk to you." George's quiet soft tone soothed his mind, but he was still not one hundred percent happy with the fact that he was supposed to or perhaps already gone on a date.

"When've I ever been calm? And why should I be?" he asked, wiping the tears off his cheeks. "I know you went out on a date tonight and couldn't even be bothered to tell me." Kevin was back to being mad. After all this time, and all the things they shared with each other, Kevin didn't understand why he went to the girls for help instead of him?

"I did go out tonight, but -" George started but Kevin pushed past him and started walking back up the path. He honestly didn't want to hear the sordid details.

"See, I knew it. Why didn't you tell me you were going to start dating. Do you think I am going to gossip about you or that I can't handle it?" Kevin yelled back. George's footsteps were so quiet, he hadn't realized he was right on his heels and he felt George's strong hand grab his wrist and whirl him around. He pulled him close against him like he had at The Sun. In the dim firelight and the light of the full moon above - George's features looked menacing, and for the very first time in his life Kevin was actually frightened of him.

"First, yes I went out tonight. Two, I know you won't gossip about me. And three I know you can handle anything. You are amazing." Kevin's eyes fluttered up to his, blinking rapidly. "You are strong and you deserve so much better in your life than what you are getting right now." George's voice was husky and gruff but then softened, and it caused a heat in Kevin he only felt when George was this close. George's eyes fixed on his and he saw something he had never seen before, and Kevin's heart made a wish. There was fire in them and it made his blood rush.

"Why did you come here?" Kevin whispered. He needed to know.

George's eyes moved from his and washed over his face, to the top of his head. His rough hand pushing a loose curl that was falling in front of his glasses back and Kevin's whole body tensed and his skin prickled at the sensation of his hand running through his hair. All he could do was fixate on George as his eyes then moved down over to his cheeks and then down to his lips. George was actively looking at his lips.

"I, I-" George stammered. "I came here to tell you; you deserve better than Jonathan." Kevin's heart sank. He already knew George hated Jonathan - this wasn't news. If this was his way of breaking them up, to come all the way up here just to say Jonathan wasn't good enough, he wasn't going to listen. Breaking free from George's embrace, Kevin shoved him in the chest, actually moving George a few feet.

"Why do you think I took time away? I don't need you telling me anything I don't already know. I am comfortable, okay? What I have with Jonathan is fine. I can deal with it." Kevin said. He was done - he didn't want to be led on anymore. Kevin continued past the fire pit and grabbed the blanket, making his way back to the sliding glass door heading into the cabin.

"You're willing to settle for fine? Or do you want someone who will love you?" George called out from the fire pit. Kevin stopped before he reached the handle.

"I will never have someone who will love me. That hope died. No one will accept me for me." Kevin softly said, his head lowered, eyes closed knowing that at any second the tears would come again. He could feel the warmth of George right behind him, that scent of his lingering heavy in the air.

"I accept you for you." George whispered.

"You would, you're my friend. But I will never find someone who *loves* me for me." Kevin said as a tear fell onto the pane of his glasses pooling on his cheeks.

"I love you." George returned, but Kevin knew he was only saying that like a friend.

"That is very sweet, but it's different. I meant not as a friend. I want someone who -" Kevin paused because he suddenly felt George's hands on his arms. George turned him around to face him again. Not wanting to let him see his tears, Kevin kept his head down, but George was not having it. Gently, George's rough fingers lifted Kevin's chin as if he were trying to lift a porcelain cup. Lightly wiping away the tears from his cheeks, George took in a deep breath.

"Who knows that you only like Pecorino Romano over Parmesan, that you hum a made-up tune while you clean dishes, that you practically twerk while you straighten up your room, or that you moan like you are having an orgasm while you eat. You want someone who knows that your favorite soaps are the ones that have lavender and rosemary in them from the farmers market because they are the perfect mix of masculine and feminine scents, that your favorite of all pastas is linguine and that you take your steak medium rare, but your burgers medium. You will drink a soda but prefer iced tea and that no matter how many times you watch that one Netflix series you still cry at the end." George's eyes were locked on his. Kevin couldn't believe that George knew all of this. Sure, they were living together but he was shocked that he had paid that much attention to him.

"How?" Kevin asked, until George stepped closer and wrapped his one arm around his waist. George brushed his nose against Kevin's and he could feel his knees buckling. The warmth of his breath washing over Kevin's lips. *Holy Shit is this real?* Kevin wasn't sure if he had fallen asleep and was having another one of those dreams or if this was a new reality.

"Because, when you love someone you learn all their quirks. Because, loving someone is about accepting them for leaving the seat up, or leaving their hair in the drain of the tub or having to listen to the endless gossip sessions. Because you are my friend, but I realized I want it to be more. Like wanting to kiss you, again." George's deep husky voice was making Kevin's head spin. His eyes fluttering, trying to comprehend what the Hell was going on.

George Nicols?

Mr. Straight?

Mr. Man's Man, was holding him in his arms and wanted to kiss him.

Again.

Kevin wasn't sure if this was a test or if this was a joke, but at this point he was willing to see. His throat was dry, and he swallowed hard trying to get his voice to actually work.

"Again? I mean it is me and I'm -" was all Kevin could get out before George's lips were on his. Kevin felt like a lit firecracker, and George just lit the fuse. As George's lips pressed against his - he felt a deep heat rising - his body electric. His kiss was soft and light, and Kevin opened his eyes to see George's. Just when he thought he was going to pull away, his hand made his way up to Kevin's head and pulled him closer, deepening the kiss.

Kevin wasn't sure he wanted to wake up from this dream and if this was truly real, he never wanted it to end. Buried hopes and dreams that were never meant to see the light of day and tossed out forever were all coming true. *He had said he loved him*, and then Kevin thought, *was it friend love or real love*? But as George's tongue slid along the seam of Kevin's lips, he didn't have to wonder anymore.

As Kevin parted his lips, he could feel George's hesitancy, but as Kevin wrapped his arms around George's neck and pressed his body against his, every ounce of hesitancy melted away. Gripping the back of George's head, Kevin deepened their kiss, allowing his tongue to dance alongside George's. A tiny throaty moan escaped George's throat and Kevin couldn't help but smile at the response. It was the most glorious sound that had ever come out of George, Kevin thought. Pulling back for a second, George's deep brown hooded eyes gazing deep into Kevin's.

"What are you smiling at?" George asked as he nipped at Kevin's lip, a rush of heat pulsing through his body.

"Can't a guy enjoy a dream coming true?" Kevin confessed, placing tiny kisses along George's jaw line. Their bodies were so close he could feel the outline of George's impressive bulge through his jeans, and Kevin was still reeling from the idea that he was turning him on. Releasing a breathy sigh, Kevin trailed kisses down George's neck as he threaded his fingers through Kevin's hair and pulled his head back to look him in the eyes again. His knees felt like they were going to buckle again from that simple gesture, but he did love having his hair pulled.

"So, you've been dreaming of me? Is that why you slept through your alarm the other morning?" George asked, his breathing heavy as he ground himself against Kevin. That dream had been amazing, Kevin wanted more, so much more, but now that it was a reality he wasn't sure if George was actually ready for that.

"Truthfully? Yes." Kevin confessed as he looked up into George's eyes, a small devilish grin spreading across his lips. George bent his head down again kissing Kevin's swollen lips.

"I knew something was up with you. If it makes you feel any better, you aren't the only one having dreams about us." George teased. Kevin's eyes widened in complete shock at the confession. Pulling away, he needed a second to wrap his brain around all of this. George having feelings and now dreaming of him. He still couldn't believe this was all true.

"I can't believe I am going to say this but, can we just talk for two minutes here? I need to understand what, and how, and why all of a sudden things with you have changed. You were literally dating Denise just last year! Like why now? Why me? Why not when I wasn't with Jonathan?" Then it dawned on him. Kevin realized he just cheated on Jonathan. "Oh my God… Jonathan! We just… you know I'm dating him! Are you making me cheat on him on purpose?" Kevin screeched. One second they were deep into making out wrapped up in a dream, and then his stupid brain made him stop. George stepped back, giving Kevin room and his expression changed. The love in his eyes shifted to that of pain.

"No, that is not why I came up here. But you are right, we definitely need to talk, because there is so much you don't know and it's not fair to you to go into this blindly." George said, holding out his hand. Kevin looked down at it, not sure he should follow him, but he knew George would never do anything to hurt him. If there was anyone in the entire world that he trusted, it was the large man right in front of him. Placing his hand in his, George led him back down to the fire pit, tossed on another log and they sat down next to each other. Kevin watched as George pulled out his cell phone, and the euphoria he was swimming in completely dissipated and now filled with a sense of dread.

"Okay, so you have a lot of questions. Good questions, and hopefully I will be able to clear a few things up." George said, his voice soft and gentle as he wrapped Kevin up in the blanket, knowing that the adrenaline running through his body was probably coming down. It was almost mind-boggling how he knew that he would start getting the chills.

"So, let's start with the elephant in the room. No, I do not like Jonathan." George stated. Kevin already knew this; it wasn't something new. He just didn't understand why and almost as if George could read his mind, he explained. "The reason being is that after last year, with him wanting an open relationship and having seen that not work out for Grace, I didn't trust him not to try and cheat on you." George explained. Kevin understood that rationale, it was the whole reason why they had broken up. He didn't want to be second best or just another option to someone. "When you two got back together, I hoped for the best for you, but I couldn't let go of this nagging feeling that he would cheat on you. So, I kinda put feelers out."

Kevin was shocked that George hadn't bothered to say anything, and the fact that he had taken it upon himself to do an investigation felt slightly wrong.

"So, you've been following my boyfriend because you think he is cheating?" Kevin asked, completely aghast that George would stoop to such hatred. But then Kevin saw him toying with his phone and George's eyes grew dark. Kevin watched as a mix of anger and pain stared back at him. Heavily sighing, George passed over his phone to Kevin. There in front of him was a picture of Jonathan with Gerald, his new stylist, making out. A burning wave rolled over Kevin's eyes as tears threatened to fall. Rage boiled his blood at the idea that Jonathan was conducting countless 'interviews' for weeks with possible new stylists, all being men.

As he looked back up into George's face, more tears fell.

"If you had these suspicions, why didn't you just tell me about it? Why keep it a secret?" Kevin questioned. George should have told him. He should have been honest and open with him.

"Would you have listened? You just said you were willing to accept whatever you got - not what you deserved." George made a good point. Kevin had been willing to accept second best because if he was going to be truthful with himself, he didn't think he deserved true love. George eased out of his seat and knelt down on his one knee and took the phone out of Kevin's hand. "You deserve so much more. You deserve to be accepted for who you are, not what you can do for someone. You need to be treasured, not be a second thought. You deserve the same love you give, not let it be tossed around like it is nothing." George explained as he removed Kevin's glasses to wipe away the tears from his dampened cheeks.

"If this was a proposal, it would be a damn good one." Kevin said, smiling at George, who actually looked embarrassed.

"I'm sorry it's not." George's voice slightly shaky as a chuckle escaped his lips. "Listen, you also asked why now. Probably because it's taken me years to realize that my person has been my friend for years. When you said that last year, I brushed it off. Then we started living together and little things I never noticed started making me see you in a different light. Some good, some bad, but it made me realize that I cared about you more than just the friends that we are. And then Brendan happened."

Kevin rolled his eyes, Brendan was a nuisance and he hoped that he never saw his face ever again, but he knew that wasn't going to be the case until he moved away again.

"I actually want to thank the guy." George admitted. Kevin couldn't believe what he was hearing and arched his brow in a quizzical glare.

"He's a monster, how can you say you want to thank him for anything?" Kevin questioned, thinking George had gone totally insane.

"Because if it wasn't for him, I never would have kissed you and perhaps I never would have realized what you meant to me."

George confessed as he leaned forward kissing Kevin again and Kevin's heart leapt. That kiss wasn't only a catalyst for Kevin but for George as well. As Kevin drove up to the cabin, he realized that he needed to decide if he actually wanted to stay with Jonathan and to get over George, or risk it all and tell him the truth. He never expected that the events of his life would change so drastically so quickly. Stuff like this only happened in his sister's books, or fairy tales, not in his life.

"So, if we hadn't kissed, would you feel this way?" Kevin asked. It was a valid question. He didn't want George to pursue a relationship just because of a kiss.

"Okay, so it's my turn to say it. Truthfully, I've been feeling this way, little by little. The kiss just brought out a desire to want to kiss you again." George's eyes staring at Kevin's lips. Involuntarily he bit his lower lip, causing George to grin. "I'm not attracted to other men. I can't picture myself being intimate with other men."

Kevin's eyes widened at the idea of the two of them actually being intimate with each other. Although, he enjoyed a handful of men in his life, George however, as far as Kevin knew – never had relations with another man before.

"Okay, well just for clarification, have you been with a man? Because you know it is slightly different than having sex with a woman." Kevin cautiously warned, garnering a tiny chuckle from George.

"No, I haven't, and yes I am aware there is a bit of a difference. And before you go down a rabbit hole, yes I will need to take this slowly, only because I don't know what to expect." George was smart, Kevin never doubted that. But the sheer fact that he trusted him to help him on this journey made Kevin feel incredible and excited that he was the one that got to share something so intimate with him. Taking a deep breath in, Kevin gathered up George's hands into his and kissed them.

"We will take this slow. I won't rush you into anything you don't want. But I need to know if there is something you have seen or done that you enjoy that you would like to try first?" Kevin asked. He needed a jumping off point and knew this was going to be a long road ahead of them.

CHAPTER NINE

George

The pounding in George's chest felt like it was being echoed off of the lake - his pulse was rushing so fast it filled his ears like heavy static. He wasn't sure whether he should tell Kevin about the other night when he had walked in on Jonathan servicing Kevin right there in the kitchen. But he didn't want to hide anything from him. Jonathan did that enough to Kevin, that George promised himself that he wouldn't hide anything from him.

"Okay, so story time and please do not be mad at me or squeamish." George started. Kevin's sweet features now twisted into a concerned glare, his eyes racing side to side, probably wondering what the heck was going to come out of his mouth. "I saw you and Jonathan in the kitchen the other day."

Kevin's jaw dropped, eyes widening in mortification. He threw his hands up over his mouth as he hoisted himself out of the chair and looked like he was going to run.

"OH MY GOD! Are you kidding me? Why didn't you say anything? OH MY GOD! Oh my God, I'm going to die. Here right here, death come take me now." Kevin yelled, collapsing down at the spot where he had finally stopped frantically pacing as he flew off the handle. George pushed himself up from his knee - now screaming in pain- and walked over to his now very-much-not-dead, but definitely-wishing-he-was, Kevin.

Standing over him, George just shook his head as his best friend pretended to be dead. "I am deceased, please let me rot in this spot. I must return to the earth and become worm food." Kevin pronounced with his eyes closed, presumably because he didn't want to look at George.

George smirked and thought, *how was he going to get Kevin to stop acting this way*. Lowering himself to the ground, he got on all fours and climbed over Kevin. The nearness of his body to Kevin's he knew would prompt a response. He was a guy after all, and most men were just sexual beasts.

"Okay, well can the talking pile of worm food look at me for a second?" George whispered. Kevin opened one eye hesitantly and George couldn't help but allow a sly grin spread across his lips. "It turned me on." Kevin's eyes widened in shock. "I ran because I wanted you. I want you to do that to me and vice versa. Your moans linger in my brain and all I want is to make you moan. It's just -" George paused. He was never insecure, but for the first time in a really long time, he was afraid to be intimate with someone and screw it up. Kevin's lips parted, waiting on what George would say. "I don't know how to service another man." Hanging his head, with his forehead touching Kevin's, he gazed deep into his best friend's deep brown eyes. Kevin's brow creased with compassion and understanding, he placed his hands on George's face bringing him in for another kiss.

"Oh, my darling. I am honored to teach you all the things. But the truth is, this may come more naturally to you than you realize." Kevin consoled, teasing him as he stole at George's bottom lip. A shiver ran down his spine and his pants felt tighter as Kevin started sucking on his lower lip, something deep within George finally let go.

Crushing his body down onto him, he heard a gasp of air and a tiny throaty moan escape Kevin's lips as he tangled his arms around George's neck. Almost on instinct, unable to control his body, his hips bucked against the smaller frame laying under him. Waves of electricity shot through his abdomen as he could feel the growing hardness in Kevin's pants. The very idea that he would be the one to taste and feel him excited George more than he had ever imagined.

Placing tiny kisses along Kevin's jaw line, he found it unexpectedly enjoyable to nuzzle against his stubbly five o'clock shadow making his way to Kevin's ear. As his lips reached his soft earlobe, he took just a tiny bit into his mouth, allowing the tip of his tongue to lave over the lower shell of it and then he bit it ever so gently. The throaty moan that escaped Kevin's mouth made his own cock become so hard so quickly. He was still shocked that this sound drove him to such a response.

"Oh my God, do it again, only this time suck hard after you bite it." Kevin begged. George grinned at the breathy request. At this point he was willing to do whatever Kevin asked for. His breathy sighs, the moaning and the squirming of him all made it feel unreal. As George ran his tongue along the outer shell of Kevin's ear, he felt him shutter under him at the sensation. Not willing to do as he commanded, he nipped at Kevin's earlobe again and he swirled the tip of his tongue around the bottom of it, soothing the harder bites he had given him. Kevin threw one leg up over George's just before he sucked bringing their bodies closer. He could feel just how hard Kevin was against his own throbbing bulge, sucking harder than before. The moan that escaped Kevin's throat was so loud he was sure someone on the lake heard him.

"Oh, I am not waiting. I know I said I would go slow," Kevin wrapped his arms around George, and with all his strength, he managed to roll all two hundred and twenty-five pounds of him onto his back as he started kissing along his chin then down his neck. "But just know if you keep doing that I will literally cum in my pants and that is not fair. I happen to like things a little rough in certain areas." Kevin was now straddling him and George looked up to him grinning. The whole scene was unreal. The moonlight, the amber lights of the fire flickering behind Kevin's frame, the smell of the grass, smoke and the coolness of the breeze and his person not willing to let him go. This was everything to him. As this feeling took him over, tears collected in his eyes.

He was free.

"Hey, hey why are you crying? Stop please, I will stop, if this is too much too soon." Kevin's worried eyes reflected back to him as his sweet friend tenderly wiped away the tear that escaped. George shook his head and grabbed Kevin's collar bringing him back down to his face.

"I'm just overwhelmed. I finally have *my person*. I've spent so long thinking it would be someone else, when all I had to do was open my eyes." George confessed. Placing a sweet kiss on George's lips, Kevin smiled at him.

"I'm just glad you did." Kevin said as his fingers danced down to George's shirt buttons, slowly unbuttoning one after the other, exposing his chest and chiseled abs. Kissing his way down over George's body, he felt like it was going to engulf in flames and combust right on the spot. Laying there in the cool damp grass, Kevin's warmth was an utter contrast and George was happy to burn right there on the spot.

Women had excited and turned him on before, but this – this was different. Everything would be now. His body felt as if it was traveling through space, almost floating and as he grasped at Kevin, it was as if he was clawing for a lifeline. The warmth of Kevin's breath across his body was nothing he ever felt before, and he wasn't sure if it was because it was Kevin, or if it was just that every nerve in his body was heightened from the new experience.

When he licked a stripe down to the top of his jeans, George's cock twitched again and he felt his boxers dampen with a bit of pre-cum seeping out. His heart raced as Kevin's nimble fingers undid his button, and the sound of the zipper sliding down made the hair on his body stand on edge. Looking down toward the devilish grin and wicked eyes, George watched as Kevin licked his lower lip before biting it, causing a rumble to echo from his chest. He was nervous but he couldn't wait. Moving back up to kiss George, Kevin's hands moved to the waist band of his jeans and hooked two fingers inside his boxers, causing George to widen his gaze.

"Say no, and I will stop." Kevin's voice became husky and deeper than George had ever heard it before. His eyes intense and commanding, this was new. George hadn't seen this side of Kevin and shockingly it was turning his blood into molten lava. No one ever made him want to just let go before. As George lifted his hips off the ground, Kevin smirked and inched back to give himself enough room to pull down George's jeans and boxers off, exposing him to the coolness of the air and grass - realizing they should have tossed down the blanket before starting this.

Kevin's eyes widened as he caught sight for the first time of the size and girth of George's hard cock. "Oh my… well, when we are ready to take things to the next level, I'm glad I have poppers."

"What are poppers?" George asked. He had never heard of that before. He wasn't sure if it was a butt plug or some kind of sex toy. As Kevin lowered his body between George's legs, he flashed another devilish smile.

"Oh, it's just a little something for me. I mean, I may have been with other men before but um… sir. You are quite impressive. I thought the whole black guy thing was a myth and those dildos were just fake." Kevin slowly wrapped his fingers around the base of George's shaft and gripped it gently, lowering his face down to the weeping head of his cock to lick the pre-cum off of it, sending shockwaves through George's whole body. "But this! You are perfection and are never allowed to leave me." Kevin added before he swirled his tongue around the crown of George's quivering dick. The guttural rumbled moan that erupted from his throat seemed to be music to Kevin's ears as he hummed on the tip. The vibration of the hum caused goosebumps all over George's body. Unable to withstand the torment, threw his head back, closing his eyes and surrendered himself to the sensation.

He'd wondered if it would be awkward to have another man touching him in such a tender way, but it wasn't. Kevin's mouth and tongue expertly worked the head of his shaft, licking and sucking the length of him as his soft hands stroked him and played with his balls. George's head spun as Kevin's one thumb pressed against the soft flesh between his balls and anus putting some pressure on the spot, and it stirred a jolt of electricity to surge through him. Lifting his head off the ground, George locked eyes with Kevin, and without further teasing, Kevin opened his drooling mouth and lowered it over his weeping cock, taking in as much of George as he could. Watching Kevin's head bobbing up and down on his length made his balls tighten, and he hadn't realized just how unbelievably quick this may be. His heart, his body – everything was smoldering in a fire George never wanted to leave.

Kevin's tongue was soft and warm as he licked and teased the head of George's shaft — which twitched and throbbed from the building orgasm — and all George could think was; he didn't want this to end. He threaded his fingers through Kevin's hair as his hips bucked involuntarily when the smaller man did his best to hollow out his cheeks to take him deeper and gagged slightly as he hit the back of his throat. Rocking his hips faster, he set the pace for them both — and when he felt the hum of a trapped moan vibrate up his length, he dropped his head back onto the ground to let out his own guttural groan.

"Kev, I am gonna cum if you do that again." George warned. But it seemed Kevin didn't care as he slipped his thumb down farther to tease his ass hole. With the spit that slid down his shaft and over his tightening balls, Kevin swirled it around and hummed. George was done – his orgasm hit harder than any other orgasm he ever experienced in his entire life and he couldn't hold back the roar that echoed through the trees. Kevin hadn't penetrated him, but the closeness and the roughly tender rhythm of the way his throat would constrict and relax as he swallowed him down had been absolute perfection. He could feel Kevin pulling him in deeper as he swallowed down the cum that had flooded his mouth, and it only prolonged his orgasm.

Shuddering with desire and the need to have him close again, George tugged on Kevin's hair – pulling him off his still weeping dick, and Kevin obliged with a wicked grin as he crawled his way back up to kiss him. At first it was a soft kiss, but George didn't want soft. He was thankful that Kevin hadn't gotten a haircut, because his fingers threaded nicely in his hair as he deepened their kiss. He wanted to know exactly what he tasted like. It was an odd thought, but he had never tasted himself. All the women he had been with would start a blow job but would never finish it, they would stop halfway and hop on top of him and he would finish while having sex.

Kevin giggled as George couldn't control himself any longer as he started to grab at his clothes, practically ripping them off of him.

"Uh sir, what do you think you are doing?" Kevin asked, but George ignored him and pulled his shirt up and out of the waist band of his pants, his hands now able to touch Kevin's taut skin. He felt the lean muscles that Kevin worked so hard to earn in the gym. The last time he had seen Kevin with his shirt up sparked a heated rush through his blood.

"You can't do what you did and think I am not going to give back." George said, placing tiny kisses down Kevin's chin, neck and down to his collar bone.

"Okay, well that is sweet, but this is your first time sweetie. I'm a fucking pro." Kevin quipped, and ground against George's still exposed groin. The same heat started back up again, causing George to shudder. A tiny chuckle escaped both their throats and George looked up at Kevin and smiled. His best friend, his comic, his true love all wrapped up in one. His heart swelled and his eyes glazed over as he stared back at the warmest person he knew. He couldn't help the tingle in his nose as more tears stung his eyes. As a tear escaped and started rolling down the side of his face, Kevin caught sight of it and kissed it away.

"I tell a joke and you cry? My jokes aren't that bad." Kevin kissed the tip of his nose and all George could do was sigh.

"I'm sorry. I'm just -" George's hand stilled on Kevin's back, wanting him so close that he wanted them fused together. "I'm afraid this isn't real. You know how you said it is a dream?" he asked. Kevin's eyes filled with love and understanding nodded. "You've been my dream. I just never could get it to come into focus." Another tear escaped George's eye as Kevin took in a shuttered breath. Finally giving in, Kevin languidly lowered his whole body onto George's. Taking the opportunity, it was George's turn to roll Kevin over and he was met with no resistance.

"I've always wanted you; I was just happy to settle as your friend." Kevin added. Love and happiness stared back into George's deep brown eyes and his heart hurt for a second. Kevin didn't have to settle anymore.

"No more settling for you. You are mine now and I will always love you, not just because you are my friend, but because I am your person, no one else's. I will not share you." George was sweet, but his words firm. He was not willing to share Kevin with anyone. Kevin blinked back as if he was being scolded, nodding quickly.

"Um, Prince Charming, you had me wanting to be with you back in high school and I never got over my first real life crush. All you needed to say was, '*Kevin you are mine,*' and I was sold." With his face being so serious, there was a part of George that couldn't take it anymore and started to laugh. "Why are you laughing at me? This is not sexy, by the way. I just confessed that I've been in love with you forever and you are laughing." Kevin scrunched up his face which only made George laugh harder. Annoyed by his laughter, Kevin attempted to push him off, but George wasn't going anywhere.

"I'm laughing because we have been idiots for years. But I'm glad we got here now." George placed tiny pecks along Kevin's jaw line and again went to kiss his ear. Releasing a sigh, Kevin gave in, not even trying to fight. Then he stilled under him.

"You have work tomorrow. You need to go." Kevin chirped, and George just shook his head, grazing his teeth along Kevin's ear which elicited a tiny, shuddered moan out of the smaller man.

"I called in a favor, no work for me. I'm off for the next four days." George sucked hard on Kevin's earlobe and got the reaction he wanted. That sigh, the same sigh of desperation and longing he heard from Kevin just two days ago. He wanted to hear it again and again.

With the exception of his shirt still being on, George was still naked from the waist down and he could feel Kevin writhing against him, wanting to be touched. *I can do this, I'm a guy, I know what feels good, how hard can this be?* George wanted to please Kevin more than anything, but he was still apprehensive. His mind raced with the knowledge that other men had done this for Kevin and probably experienced similar mind-blowing blow jobs like the one Kevin performed for him. George wanted that for him. He wanted to erase every other man who entered into Kevin's life and needed him to forget them.

The possessive beast lurking in his chest was something new, but then again, so was this. George let the beast take over him as he started kissing down Kevin's neck, stopping at his pulse point, he sucked hard. Kevin let out a breathy sigh, and George thought to himself, *not good enough*. Sucking harder this time, he wanted to leave a mark. *He's mine and I don't care who sees*. Kevin's fingers raked across George's back, digging his nails into George's taut skin and a rumble emerged from his chest.

As George continued punishing Kevin's skin moving further down to his shirt, he hoisted himself up as Kevin did earlier, now straddling him. Slowly, he yanked at the shirt Kevin was wearing and finally removed his own shirt, leaving himself completely naked. Kevin stared up to him as he reached up his hands, finding purchase on George's chest and padded his thumbs over his nipples, teasing them as he bit his lower lip.

The sensation sent a rush of heat to George's semi-hard cock and there was no doubt how the man below him excited him and turned him on. Kevin bucked his hips up. George could feel just how deeply aroused he was and his heart sung. He hadn't caught a full sight of Kevin so he wasn't sure just how big he was but based on how he felt in the joggers against George's ass, this was going to be interesting.

"We really should have grabbed that blanket. This grass is cold, why didn't you say anything?" Kevin hissed, still trying to adjust to the coolness. Grinning down to him, George moved off of him and walked back to the fire pit, grabbing the blanket.

"Because I was about to get my dick sucked. I wasn't about to say stop, it's cold. Besides I did cold weather training in Norway. A little bit of cold grass wasn't going to bother me." George said, placing the blanket down next to Kevin and extending his hand out to him to help him up. Pulling him flush to his naked self, George's body tingled at the closeness of Kevin's flesh to his and his blood rushed. Running his hands over Kevin's body, he explored his skin that was turning to gooseflesh under the pads of his fingers and Kevin's breath caught as his fingers went lower to his waist band.

Still not sure he was ready. George wrapped his arms around Kevin's waist and let his hands rest along the back of Kevin's joggers.

"You don't have to. If we have four days, we can take this slow. There is a jacuzzi we can just sit and enjoy. I'm really okay if you aren't ready." Kevin whispered against his lips. George's heart fluttered. He wanted to, he was just scared of messing it up.

"I want to do this, I -" George's voice quivered with hesitation.

"Hey, look at me." Kevin shook his head. "We aren't gonna do this tonight, okay. I don't want any hesitation, or concern. I want you to do this when you are ready. But if you can just grab my ass right now, that might hold me over." Kevin's voice was soft and endearing. Only his best friend would know how he felt. Only someone who loved him with utter and complete devotion in their heart would understand.

"If I grab your ass, I won't stop there." George explained as he lowered his fingers to the back of Kevin's waist band teasing the tips of his fingers inside, garnering a gasp from Kevin's lips and he shook his head.

"No, I will stay strong. I will not let you go further than just squeezing my ass. I promise." Kevin said with conviction in his voice. However, George was completely skeptical. Slipping his large rough hands down onto Kevin's bare ass, he was shocked to find that Kevin wasn't wearing underwear. "What? I like going commando. I wasn't expecting anyone up here. I was soul-searching, remember?"

"I remember. Have you finished your soul-searching?" George asked, kneading Kevin's ass cheeks and felt him literally melting in his hands. Through heavy-lidded, smoky eyes, Kevin smiled back, licking his lips and then biting them before nodding *yes*.

"Mm hm. All done, I know what I want." Kevin's breathy words breezed across George's lip and he couldn't help but smile.

"Good. Because I wasn't leaving here until you were mine." George said and Kevin melted right there in his arms and the beast in his chest settled and purred for joy.

CHAPTER TEN

Kevin

As the sunlight streamed in through the light lacy curtains of the bedroom window, Kevin stirred from the heat it was generating. Only the windows were cracked just a hair, and his bare skin prickled from the coolness of the room on his exposed skin above the covers. He realized the heat wasn't coming from the sun but the large body behind him with their arm resting against his middle.

Flashes of the night before raced across his mind as he realized it hadn't been a dream. This was reality. As he looked down at George's chocolate hued arm, hung in contrast to his peaches and cream mid-section, and felt himself getting aroused. *It was real*. George drove all the way up here to confess how he felt, to convince him to leave

Jonathan (very little convincing was necessary after he saw the pictures) and to be his.

Fairy tales were not just fiction. It was real. Time and time again for his friends and family. But Kevin never thought it possible for himself until last night. To be in love with someone for so long, and for them to finally be on the same page, was only something he reserved for people like his sister. Grace and Jim making foolish teenage mistakes, and then the bad decision duo - Hank and Denise were no different. The only ones who seemed to have it right from the start seemed to be Nikki and Mike. Their love story was sweet; he had won her over from another woman Nikki was dating at the time.

But now that Kevin looked at his and George's story, it wasn't too far off from a fairy tale as well. Kevin's long pining after George for years and giving up all hopes. George finally realizing that the one he wanted to be with was his best friend all along. It was something right out of the pages of one of Grace's friends to lovers romances. And then he remembered Grace. She had lied to him, that sneaky little minx. There was no way, this was all a coincidence. Knowing her, she and his bitches helped with all this. A part of him wanted to be pissed off at them, but as George's arm tightened around Kevin and snuggled deeper into his back – *how could he be pissed?*

He was in the arms of the man of his dreams. His every wish he dared to dream had come true in one night. Closing his eyes and taking a deep breath in, Kevin settled deeper into George's arms. He never wanted to leave this space for fear of this whole thing not being real. But his bladder was screaming for him to go.

Trying to be quiet and not disturb George, he tried shifting just a smidge onto his back but George just pulled him closer.

"Where are you going? I am not ready to let you go." George whispered, his breath warm on Kevin's neck. He felt a tingling in his belly and knew it was a matter of seconds before his dick would be rock hard.

"I need to use the bathroom, but I can come back and join you once I'm done." Kevin admitted, but he knew he had nothing to hide. George already knew his habits. The first thing he did was run to the bathroom in the morning and do what he needed to. Feeling George's arm loosen, Kevin rolled himself out of the king-size bed (thank you Grace for the oversized bed), throwing on his glasses and ran naked into the ensuite. He heard George's chuckling from the bedroom and then the slight padding of his feet walking across the room as George stood just outside the doorway.

Kevin's routine was the same every morning. Pee, wash hands, brush teeth, check for crow's feet, then hop in the shower, but now that George was waiting on the other side of the door he wasn't sure he would do all of that. So, he decided on the first three and quickly opened the door to a very handsome and also very naked George.

"What? You aren't the only one who needs the bathroom and I wasn't sure I wanted to stroll around the cabin naked looking for another bathroom." Moving to one side, Kevin let him pass and shut the door behind him. The truth was he didn't know whether he should climb back into bed or toss his joggers back on and start coffee. Coffee…coffee first and also to send a text to his rotten misleading sister.

"I'm gonna go start the coffee, I'll be right back." Kevin said through the door.

"Sounds great. And tell Grace I said 'hi'." George's voice muffled through the door.

There was nothing he would ever get past George. Heading out to the expansive kitchen/living space, Kevin needed to be honest with himself. This wasn't just some cabin. It was a ridiculously large chalet that his sister went and invested a ludicrous amount of money into so that she could rent it out and use it for yet another family retreat. He remembered how she bought the house for pennies on the dollar. It was run down, needed a ton of work just like the shore house had, and she expanded it. As he walked into the knotty dark-stained pine kitchen, he went over and started making a full pot of coffee for the two of them.

Grabbing his phone off the table from where he left it the night before, he found there were a bunch of video messages and texts. One from George before he arrived, and the rest were all call requests and messages from this morning till now. His group *Bitches be Bitches*, consisting of Grace, Nikki and Denise tried calling around nine a.m. and his initial thought was to ignore them. But since he had a few minutes, he figured he would call the traitors.

Hitting the phone icon on the group, he waited for all of two seconds before all three faces were on his screen.

"Moooooorning." Denise drawled, it was taking everything in him not to be grinning from ear to ear.

"What were the three of you thinking?" All three women's excited faces instantly changed as he watched their expressions alter from hopefulness to disappointment. "How could you do this to me!" Kevin spat. He was going to make them suffer.

"Sweetie, listen we only meant well." Nikki retorted, her brows furrowed.

"And you! You told me that he was going on a date. You lied to me! You broke my heart on purpose." Kevin was looking directly at Grace who was now blushing and clearly felt guilty based on the look she was giving him.

"I had to, we all had to. Why are you mad at us? Didn't George go up there and talk to you about his feelings?" Grace questioned, and his heart leapt at knowing not twenty feet away was everything he hoped for, but he was gonna make them pay.

"He did." Denise arched her brow as she cast a discerning gaze at him. Kevin went on, "Did you think it was going to change how I felt about Jonathan?" that got Grace to roll her eyes. "This was all of you meddling into my life by trying to break up me and Jonathan!" Nikki gave an unapologetic eyebrow raise. "Do you think I am that easily fooled? I already knew he couldn't stand Jonathan and you made him use it against me! You should all be ashamed." Kevin said, but there faces didn't seem to now be buying it. He watched as their brows softened, and he looked at the screen with his face on it and saw George standing behind him, smiling.

"Morning ladies." George said, before the chorus of screams and laughter erupted on the other end of the call.

"Morning to you, Sir. I forgot how good you look without your shirt." Denise said and a muffled '*hey*' came from the background, Hank clearly hearing what she said. Not two seconds later Hank, who was dressed only in a towel, appeared behind Denise looking down at the screen.

"Oh well it's about damn time. Morning fellas. See, and you were worried it wouldn't work." Hank kissed Denise, then waved with his one free hand as his other was holding his towel from slipping. Kevin wouldn't have minded if it had. Part of him was always curious, but it seemed that George must have been reading his mind as he leaned over Kevin's back to see what was going on.

"Oh my God, how many of you were in on this?" Kevin looked at the screen and now Mike's head popped in behind Nikki.

"All of us." Jim yelled from somewhere behind Grace, prompting everyone to laugh. Only Kevin was now truly perturbed. Not just with his sister but all of his friends. Whirling around to face George, who was now the one blinking rapidly at Kevin's angry expression, he shrugged looking incredibly guilty.

"What? They just wanted to see you happy. Could you blame them?" George cooed as he slowly wound his arms around Kevin and the chorus of aws on the other end of the phone caused Kevin to roll his eyes.

"Yes, I can. And I blame you too. You could have just told me how you felt." Kevin explained and a small smile spread across George's lips.

"Would you have listened?" Mike asked. Kevin had completely forgotten about the call the second George had wrapped his arms around him. *He is going to be dangerous if I get lost in his eyes and arms like this*, Kevin thought to himself. He needed to end this call because all he wanted right now was a coffee and a good morning kiss from George.

Whirling back around now all six of his friends and family were on screen watching everything unfold right in front of them, hanging on every word.

"Alright you busy bodies, you won, okay? I listened and I got what I have always wanted, now let us go. I have a boyfriend to kiss." Kevin said to another round of awes from the ladies and he hung up the call. Sighing, Kevin felt all of his emotions all at once. As George wrapped his arms around Kevin from behind, he kissed the back of his neck and he couldn't help but melt again. George was setting tiny flames along his neck, his muscles and bones in Kevin's neck became mush with every brush of his lips against his skin. His head fell back onto George's shoulder as his large hands slowly made their way down his abdomen.

"Please don't stop this time. I know I said slow but my God, please." Kevin begged as George nipped at the soft skin between his neck and shoulder.

"Oh, I have no intention of stopping, I still want my moan." George promised as his fingers nimbly slid into Kevin's joggers and he shuddered at the feel of them on his bare skin. There was no hesitation this time from George as his fingertips brushed gently along the base of his shaft and Kevin was so glad he had gotten that wax the other day.

George's hands were rough against the sensitive skin of his balls as he cupped them in his left hand and squeezed lightly, curling the fingers of his right hand around his engorged length. Kevin's shaft twitched from the pressure as the larger man's hand slid up his length, sending sparks of electricity — just as intense as the night before —

through him as George's thumb swept over the head of his cock, and smeared the pre-cum that had started to leak out from his earlier kisses. Kevin couldn't help it — his hips bucked from the sensation, and he thrust his length into George's strong hand.

"Are you that desperate for me?" George kissed the other side of his neck and moved up to Kevin's ear. Reaching behind him, he grabbed George's hips and pulled them against him, and he could feel that he was just as hard as he was the night before.

"God, yes. Always." Kevin moaned as George slowly started stroking him. He was methodical, slow and smooth, languid strokes as George nipped and sucked on Kevin's earlobe, releasing it over and over again with a pop. His breath hitched when George pulled gently on his balls and then squeezed them as George's other hand started picking up the pace.

"Tell me you want me." George commanded, and Kevin felt a tightening in his belly and a shiver down his spine.

"Oh God, I want you. I've always wanted you." Kevin confirmed. He couldn't lie. It was all true, he had wanted him since the second he had met him all those years ago. With that tiny bit of encouragement George picked up his pace, dragging the tiny droplets of cum weeping out down the length of his dick making his strokes easier to glide up and down.

"You need me." George demanded, his breath warm on Kevin's neck. He wasn't wrong, Kevin *did* need him. He needed him more than air, more than water. It was as if he was life itself. And Kevin felt his orgasm a breath away. He wanted him inside him. No, he craved him to be inside him, but that would have to be a different day, because his poppers were hidden at home and the idea of him riding George's large cock caused a throaty moan to escape his throat.

"Do it again, moan for me." George's commanding tone drove him just seconds away, and then he did the thing he hadn't expected yet: George started rutting against him. Only two pieces of fabric kept him from actually fucking him right there in the kitchen. And that was it. All of Kevin's senses were on edge, and just when he was sure he couldn't take anymore George said, "Cum for me, love." And that was it. Every part of Kevin exploded and the moans that ripped from his throat echoed in the cathedral ceilings as ropes of cum streamed out of his oversensitive dick. His pants were a mess, but he didn't care. He was having a hard time staying on his feet and trying to catch his breath.

"God I want you right now." George said, still rutting against Kevin's ass and at this point he didn't care. He had a condom in his wallet sitting right there on the counter but he wasn't sure it would fit over George's cock. Kevin wore a large but George was like a magnum XL or something just as absolutely ridiculous.

"Condom, please tell me you have a condom!" Kevin asked in between still catching his breath and George still stroking him. George's hands and hips stilled and dropped his head on Kevin's shoulder.

"I didn't think we would be doing this and I took mine out of my wallet because of the expiration date." George kissed the back of Kevin's neck and the two men sighed collectively.

"Yeah well I hadn't thought to prep before I came up here, so if we did, it would be a little messy and I can't have that for our first time." Kevin said, trying to look back at George. Raising his head, George leaned over and kissed him on the lips.

"I appreciate that. It will be better once we get home. We can leave and just hide out at home for the next couple of days." George suggested, but Kevin was actually enjoying it up here in the solitude of the woods. He would never actually tell people that - but he did. He had found a new appreciation for this place. As George carefully pulled his cum covered hands out of Kevin's pants, Kevin turned and looked up at him. With George being six foot two and Kevin only being five feet eleven inches tall, he had him by a few inches and it was actually nice to have to look up at him.

"I can finish you off and then take a shower?" Kevin offered, and for a few seconds George thought about it.

"Or you can do that in the shower?" George asked, placing a tiny kiss on Kevin's nose. That sounded like a solid plan. With coffee forgotten, George led the way to the bathroom and Kevin, like the good little puppy he was for George, followed.

The next several days flew by so fast Kevin had been pouting all morning long. While making his cup of coffee, George glanced over to him as he was scrolling through his phone and nudged his shoulder as he sat down on the stool next to him.

"I don't know why you are all pissy. We are heading home, it's no different than being here. And honestly, I'd like to put on a different outfit every day instead of washing this one over and over." He said, taking his first sip of coffee.

"I told you we could have gone to the outlets and gotten you some clothes for a major discount and we could have gotten other stuff while we were out." Kevin finally had a smile on his face as he wiggled his eyebrows. They may not have actually engaged in sex yet, but all the other extracurricular activities were sublimely delicious. It only meant there was so much more to look forward to once they did get home.

Yet, at the same time he knew George wasn't actually ready for that yet. Kevin sat him down and explained his normal routine of how he prepped before having anal sex. Explaining it to George in a very clinical manner so that he understood. He knew that this was something he could appreciate since he was such a routine regimented individual. Due to Kevin's lack of sexual experiences with a woman, he only knew what he needed to do to have clean and safe sex. He hated messy sex; it completely grossed him out. He explained to George that he enjoyed being a 'power bottom' and didn't like to make his partners messy.

The elephant in the room was that Kevin still had to face Jonathan. Part of him wanted to call his cheating out, and another part of him wanted to tell him that he didn't see a future with him, which they both knew was never going to happen. But at the same time, he kind of wanted him to suffer. How long did he think he could get away with this? It felt that since they got back together, Jonathan spent a good portion of his time love bombing him, making Kevin wonder if anything he said was truly sincere, or if it was just the act of a guilty conscience.

The idea of him being with other men while dating Kevin made him cringe and his skin crawl. If he hadn't just gone for his annual check-up, he would be running to his doctor's office immediately to have a bunch of tests to make sure he was clean. Fortunately, all his blood work had come back clean from his visit last week. He also was a massive proponent of safe sex when dating.

Leaning over and resting his head on George's shoulder, he looked out of the window at the expanse of the lake and the trees. With the cooler weather, the colors were starting to change and the simple greens were now more orange, red and yellows peeking through as the breeze blew through them.

"I really love it up here." Kevin said. George nodded in agreement. "I don't want to go back. If we go back, we have to go back to reality. Let's just stay up here forever." Kevin sulked. Kissing the top of Kevin's head, George went over and checked his own phone.

"Sadly, we can't, but luckily we are not heading home to empty bellies. Your mother has invited us for dinner and my parents are invited as well." George chuckled and showed Kevin that text.

The idea that his mother was already orchestrating family dinners was just insane. It had only been a few days, and yes they were all friends, including their parents, but he just couldn't get over how quickly everything seemed to be moving.

"See! We need to stay here and not go home. My mother is going to be intolerable. I have literally been ignoring every text she has sent." Kevin ran his fingers through his still damp hair from his shower and felt like crawling back into the bed he just made in preparation for heading home. George stood next to him and Kevin could feel his gaze on him. He didn't need to see that George was giving him that comforting glance that he always gave him whenever he had to do something he didn't want.

"Listen, nothing has changed okay. We are still best friends, we are still roommates, it's just that it now comes with incredible perks. I'm not going to let this change my dynamic with you." George consoled, as he took his empty mug over to the sink and started washing it. Kevin knew he was right.

"I know. It's just that they are gonna make a fuss now." Kevin said, bringing over his own mug and handing it to George to wash while he dried the clean one. This simple tiny act was reminiscent of an old couple helping each other out, making his heart swell a bit.

"So let her, she is happy. Hell, my mother is over the moon. She's already asking me about whether you will be coming to Thanksgiving dinner or if we will be there for dessert." George laughed. "I think she forgets that I may have to work. But you see they're just happy for us, and I'm not gonna rain on their parade. And you shouldn't either." George said, passing him the second now clean mug to dry. Kevin hadn't even thought past this weekend. How much of their lives would change? Splitting holidays with families just seemed unreal to him. Was their relationship truly one that would last? What happens if another woman comes along and George leaves him for her? His mind raced at all the negative intrusive thoughts.

George noticed his silence and took the mug and dish towel out of his hand. Wrapping his arms around him, he pulled Kevin in for a tight embrace.

"What awful ideas are running around through your brain?" he asked. Kevin's eyes snapped up to his. *Was he psychic?*

"How do you do that?" Kevin questioned, shaking his head in astonishment.

"Because you, Sir, can't hide anything with your face. What's going on?" George asked, before placing a gentle peck on his nose. Kevin looked back at him and then threw his arms around him, hugging him tightly.

"I'm just worried that you'll meet some woman and decide that I'm just your friend that you got to try out being intimate with." Kevin's stomach wrenched with the idea that any morning this would all go away. But then George pulled back and lifted Kevin's chin up so he could gaze deep into his eyes, instantly melting Kevin's fears with just a simple glance.

"Kev, when I said you are my person I meant it. You are who I want to be with. I only feel like myself around you. So, if it will make you feel better, will you be my boyfriend?" George asked. It sounded ridiculous. Denise and Grace both said how weird it had been for them to refer to their partners as boyfriends because of their ages and now he understood.

"How about we just be each other's person. Like we always have been." Kevin smiled, then pulled George in for a soft kiss. "But if Brendan is around you ARE my big bad boyfriend that will arrest him for being stupid." He added with a coyish grin. Closing his eyes and shaking his head, George just laughed.

"I can't arrest people for being stupid. Doing stupid illegal things, yes. But not for being stupid." George scolded.

"Fine, hopefully he will do something incredibly dumb and I will be able to watch you put him away." Kevin smiled, and he thought that that would be a great sight to see.

CHAPTER ELEVEN

Grace

What do you mean, you aren't coming over for pizza and cupcakes after trick or treating? It's Halloween, I always host Halloween!" Grace argued, still stunned that Kevin was blowing her off. Halloween pizza and cupcakes was a tradition since they were kids. Their mother had done it that one year when Halloween got rained out, and now it was Grace's turn since she had her own kids.

"I can come over for a little bit, but I am not going to pass up money. And besides it's The Sun. It's a Friday night. And since I'm buying the cabin off of you, I need to make extra cash." Kevin explained. The Sunday he and George came back from their romance fest over a month ago, he asked Grace if he could buy it. She had the shore house and rarely went up to the cabin, and because it held such an amazing meaning to him, he thought he would buy it.

"I know, but it's Halloween and besides I gave you a rock-bottom price on it. It's not my fault that the properties around it made it so pricey." Grace said as she stood on the step ladder, trying to hang up fake cobwebs along the wide doorway leading into the living room. As Kevin offered Grace his hand to come down the ladder, Jim came stomping into the hallway with another orange and black tub no doubt filled with more Halloween decorations.

"Grace, let's be honest, that cabin isn't a cabin, it's practically a resort home. And after talking to one of your neighbors up there, once you did the remodel everyone else's looked awful so you kind of set off a chain reaction and they all went bigger and better." Jim said.

"Okay but see, worth the value!" Grace retorted as she moved the step ladder over to keep hanging up cobwebs. Kevin walked over to the tubs and grabbed a large fake spider for her to hang in the middle of the doorframe. "Is George working that night? I know it's usually all hands-on deck." Grace asked.

Everyone was happy for them. Kevin and George were an actual thing and Grace wasn't sure what magic George spun over Kevin, but he actually gave the impression to be lighter making it much easier to talk to him. A stark contrast from how he had been with Jonathan. Grace had to give it to Kevin. He handled the entire affair beautifully, with her assistance, of course.

After returning from the Poconos, Kevin appeared in the doorway to her office to chat asking for her help in how he should broach the whole subject.

"Well, well, well. Look what the cat dragged in." Grace said, sitting at her desk still trying to work on her current romance, but she had finally hit a brick wall. She still wasn't sure what to do with her two female main characters that seemed to have reached a happy place and she knew that something else needed to happen.

Kevin just smirked at her and she wasn't sure if he was gonna start an argument or not.

"Did you talk with Mommy?" Kevin asked. He already knew the answer so she wasn't sure why he was even asking.

"Yes, so you want to know how to handle Jonathan?" Grace arched her brow, already knowing that this was something he didn't want to do. "I can always go over there and tell him we all know he is a lying, cheating asshole and he doesn't deserve you and that you are going to be with someone who does." Grace offered, which got a laugh out of Kevin.

"No, I should handle this myself. I just don't want to make a massive deal about it." Kevin said, as he finally sat down on the

loveseat and lounged back allowing his legs to dangle over the one arm rest.

"So, then just don't even bring up the affair. I would just say that you know he is a free spirit and that it is best that you let him go because it isn't fair for you to keep him in a relationship. That you want him to be free to live his life and do whatever he wants with whoever he wants. Act like it's an act of mercy. You're setting him free." Grace said, knowing that this should work after everything that had happened with Hank. And although that went completely sideways, it did wind up working out in the end.

"Yeah well, what happens when he fights me on it? Do I show him the pictures then?" Kevin asked, flipping through his phone still looking at the pictures that George sent to him as back up in case Jonathan tried to deny it. He scoffed audibly at the pictures.

"Honestly, just be like, I feel like you haven't been your true self for the past couple of months and I don't want to see you suffer just because I want a committed relationship. I want you to be you. You know that bullshit. Make it about him, and if he pushes then say listen I know about the affair and I'm okay with it. I just want you to be happy and I know you aren't happy with just me. He's a narcissist, just act like you are doing him a favor." Grace knew how to handle narcissists better than anyone. Kevin sat there bobbing his head in agreement, and deep down inside he must have known she was right.

"Yeah, okay. So besides that, I want to talk to you about the cabin." He said rather sheepishly and she didn't like his tone. Did they break something? Did they have sex on every surface in the house? Glaring at him with the same look her mother would give them, she prepared for the worst. "I want to buy it."

Well, that was not what she expected him to say. He wanted to buy property? He had been hoarding his money for years and probably had enough to at least put up half the money for the house. She was just shocked that he wanted to buy it off of her.

"Uh, okay. Why? I mean I love that house, but why there? I have two properties here in town you can easily buy off me, and for cheaper because they are smaller. Why the cabin?" Grace asked, but she had a gut feeling she knew already. As Kevin took a deep breath in and then let it out, she knew.

"Because I want a home for George and I that has meaning." Kevin said, his big brown eyes glazed over and Grace felt that familiar tingle in her nose right before she was going to start crying. "It's where he told me he loved me." He whispered, and Grace lost it.

"Sold!" Grace said, as Kevin practically fell off the loveseat. Scrambling to get back up, with tears in his eyes, he reached across and hugged her as tight as he could.

"Oh my God. Seriously? I thought you were gonna haggle the shit out of me." Kevin wept, kissing Grace's face over and over as the two of them laughed. She couldn't think of a better thing than the two of them having a home away from home. Although she loved the cabin, her love for the shore house was greater because it was where she and Jim rekindled their lives together.

"When something means as much as it does, it's hard to haggle when it comes to love. Never argue the price, it's not worth it. I would've still thrown myself in front of that fucking car to save Jim's life all over again." Grace said, but Kevin just glared at her.

"That psycho was aiming for you!" He exclaimed, as if she didn't know that already.

"Yes, but I pushed him out of the way so he would be safe. I could have thrown him in front of the car. I saw who was behind the wheel. I could've been like, your ex-wife, your circus, but I didn't." Grace tried explaining her rationale, but the truth was that she would do anything to save any one of her friends or family. Kevin just shook his head at Grace.

"Okay, so, in all seriousness, how much is the house worth so I can figure out how much to pull from my savings... five hundred thousand, six?" Kevin's questioning tone giddy with the idea that the house would be his quickly as he went through his phone. Grace just grimaced because she just had the house appraised.

"One point three?" Grace winced, knowing Kevin would blow his top. But Kevin looked up, surprised and actually giddy.

"Thousand? Didn't you buy it for more?" Kevin questioned, and Grace watched as he noticed the worried look on her face. The jovial look he had mere seconds before withered away to the sudden realization. "MILLION? I can't afford a million-dollar house! You are gonna make me buy it for a million dollars? I'm your brother!" Kevin's face was actively turning green.

"Listen, I sunk a ton of money into that house for years, between the extensions, upgrades, landscaping… all that stuff is not cheap. And it's right on the lake, that is prime real estate. Diane said that one of the renters offered two million for it." Grace tried explaining, but Kevin was not hearing it.

"I'm your BROTHER! I'm not Joe Schmoe looking for a hide-away spot. I want this to be our home when George retires. He has been hinting about it since he broke his ankle last year. Now that we are together, I figured, maybe we could just move up there once he does." Kevin explained and it was taking everything within Grace not to break down and cry again. The sweetness that Kevin had in his heart to want to spend his savings in wanting to buy a place just for them was amazing. But at the same time, she realized he wouldn't be just around the corner anymore. It would be a two-hour drive to see them.

"You know Mommy is gonna be heartbroken that you want to move away?" Grace asked, trying her best to blink back tears of joy for her brother. He had finally found somewhere and someone he found peace with. How could she say no?

"Oh, I am well aware of the meltdown she is going to have. But don't change the subject. Can you please lower the price on it?" Kevin asked with hope in his voice. Getting up from her chair, she pulled him up off the couch and hugged her brother.

"Let me talk it over with Jim and I will come up with a decent enough price." Grace said. The truth was that she was going to sell it to him for a song. He was her brother after all, and he deserved all the happiness in the world.

The weather had turned much colder the last week in October and all the leaves were bright oranges, reds and yellows with the only green were the large pines in town. As Grace sat outside on the front porch drinking her coffee that morning wrapped up in her favorite green blanket, she watched as people were coming and going along Walnut Avenue.

Jim and George had gone out for an early run, leaving her behind with the kids still in bed sleeping. These tiny moments made her extremely happy that she got to enjoy the quiet before the chaos exploded in the house. Taking another sip of her coffee, she heard the front door creak open and Katie popped her head outside and smiled a sleepy grin at Grace.

"Hey, good morning sunshine. I was expecting you to be sleeping a little later." Grace said as the gorgeous teen walked out holding her own coffee mug. Shuffling out onto the deck in a pair of slippers and a fuzzy robe Grace had gotten her last Christmas, Katie sat down and took a sip of her coffee.

"Nah, I couldn't sleep. I know I'm weird for a teen." Katie said, blowing on her coffee as tiny wisps of steam swirled around her lips. Grace smiled. She was the same way at her age. Grace was a morning bird, up and early to catch that worm.

"I was the same way at your age. So, what's new in the land of Katie? How was work yesterday?" Grace had come to enjoy the relationship she was developing with the girls. She wasn't trying to replace Liz in any way, but after everything that happened, Grace knew they needed a maternal person in their lives. She treated them no different than her own sons. If they were precious to Jim, they would be precious to Grace.

After meeting Katie and Vivian two years before, it was clear that Liz hadn't been the parent they needed, and Jim adopted the function of being both mom and dad. When Katie expressed a desire to write, it made Grace's soul soar. Although she knew that Katie had read

Caroline's Lost, much to Jim's dismay, she told Grace that it inspired her to want to write but was hesitant to tell Jim. Grace knew what the teen was doing. Katie hoped that she could advocate to Jim on her behalf to allow her to write her own romance novel. Honored beyond all belief, Grace practically tripped over her own feet to help Katie out. Although she knew it was completely out of line, she didn't ask. That night, tangled in his arms, Grace told him that she was going to help Katie write it. And although he tried to protest, Jim eventually caved in.

"It was fine, I was on homework duty at the rec center, so I was helping the little kids with their assignments. I actually got asked by a mom to help with tutoring for extra cash on the side. I told her I would let her know." Katie said with a big smile on her face. Grace thought she would make an amazing kindergarten teacher, or at least in the younger grades because of how good she was with Colin.

"Well, that's amazing. A little extra cash is always good. Who's the family?" Grace asked before taking a sip of coffee.

"Um, the kid's name is Brendan Moser." Katie said, and Grace nearly choked on her coffee.

"I'm sorry, who?" Grace asked. Wanting to make sure she heard this right.

"Brendan, he's super cute. Kinda shy. I think he's new in town. He mentioned that his parents are split and he lives with mom, but she lets his dad see them sometimes. I think it's a whole custody thing. He's like Colin's age so it might be hard for him." Katie said. Grace blinked repeatedly. She didn't want Katie anywhere near Brendan Moser. He was a despicable person, but she felt bad for his ex-wife and kids.

"Why don't we do this… let's have his mom and Brendan come here and let me meet them. I want to get to know who they are first before you say yes to anything." Grace said. This was the perfect opportunity to meet the poor soul that had fallen in love with such an awful human, and she could find out a little more about him. Maybe the wife and kids were great, but either way, she was not going to allow Katie or any of her kids near that miserable lump of flesh.

As Grace pulled the bat sugar cookies out of the oven, the doorbell rang and she heard the stomping of feet come scrambling down the stairs.

"I got it!" Katie yelled, and Grace smiled thinking to herself, *'showtime'*.

Walking out of the kitchen and into her center hall, she saw a very tired looking woman with muted blonde hair wearing a crumpled suit standing next to a boy that was practically the exact image of Brendan Moser when he was eight years old. Grace's heart immediately went out to the woman in front of her. She could actually feel the exhaustion coming off of her from where she was standing in her front hall.

"Hi, I'm Grace Wooley, Katie's stepmom. Come in." Grace held her hand out and the woman sighed as she saw the warm smile Grace placed on her face. It seemed that she needed that simple act of kindness. Colin must have heard the door and poked his head out of the TV room, running right over to the little boy standing there just looking all around the house at the Halloween decorations.

"Hi, I'm Colin, you want to come play video games with me?" Colin asked, Grace just smiled and shook her head. *Leave it to Colin to just introduce himself and say hey come play*, she thought. Grace looked to the woman, who still hadn't introduced herself and just nodded that it was okay, hoping that she would get the chance to talk to her alone. As the mother and child exchanged silent glances, Grace's stomach turned as she could only imagine if these two needed to learn how to communicate with each other in silence living with Brendan. He seemed like the type of jerk that would expect silence in his home.

As the boys went off into the TV room, Grace smiled at the woman, still waiting on her to introduce herself. Katie must have noticed the odd tension because she instantly spoke up.

"Grace, this is Brendan's mom, Kelly Moser." Katie said, but the woman shook her head.

"I'm sorry, it's Kelly Linchal, Moser was my married name. I got my maiden name back in the divorce." Kelly said, and Grace didn't miss the amount of loathing she had in just saying the name Moser. Grace wanted to keep playing dumb, but something in her didn't want to either. She hated deception, but she had learned from her father that in order to get information you need sometimes you must be calculated in what you say.

"Ah, well I've been divorced, so I know what that is like. You just moved into Toselle Park, right?" Grace was just trying to connect with her. She could see the reservations in her pale-tired eyes. She had been fortunate to have family and friends to be there for her and the boys had been easy. To imagine having to co-parent with Brendan sounded like the most horrific thing one could deal with.

"Yes. After my divorce, I was forced into selling our home and relocating to accommodate my ex-husband." Kelly said, looking down at herself, trying to press out the wrinkles in her suit. The poor thing was nervous. Grace smiled at her and knew she needed to get Kelly to relax.

"Gotcha, can I get you a cup of coffee, tea, water?" Grace asked. If there was anything she knew, it was that nothing helped to steal her nerves better than a cup of tea. Or a shot of vodka.

"A tea would be lovely actually." Kelly muttered with a weary smile and followed Grace into the kitchen with Katie bringing up the rear. As she filled the kettle, Grace turned to Katie.

"Hey Katie, why don't you go hang out with the boys. That way if everything goes well, you and Brendan will have a good rapport going already." Grace said with a little nod in the direction of the TV room. With a wink, Katie nodded in agreement and headed off to spend time with the two younger kids. Turning back to Kelly, Grace smiled again and grabbed two mugs out of the cupboard and grabbed her box of different teas, offering for Kelly to pick out whichever one she wanted.

"So, Kelly, how are you adjusting to Toselle Park? You mentioned you had to move here because of your divorce?" Grace asked. She watched as Kelly sighed in annoyance.

"Most of the people are fine. Everyone has been really great at welcoming me and my kids. I have an older daughter in middle school." Kelly said with a bit of hesitation.

"And the ex-husband, how has the co-parenting been going? I know how that can be difficult at times." Grace didn't want to push her too hard.

"Ugh, well that is the only downfall, right? The ex. I don't know if you know him. Brendan Moser? He grew up here in town." Kelly asked, clearly she could see through Grace's veiled attempt to be discrete. Slowly bobbing her head in confirmation, Grace wasn't sure just what she could say and what she couldn't. "I figured as much, not that I blame you for being cautious for Katie. He is a miserable son of a bitch." Kelly said, adding honey to her tea before taking a sip.

"Yeah, we went to school together. I'm sorry I wasn't straight forward with you right off the bat. But my family has history with him and his family." Grace said, as she pulled out a bundt loaf she had made just that morning.

"Oh, I have heard all the stories and even knew who all of you were before I moved here. He used to stare at the yearbook going on and on about how great he was before the injury. I look back now and realize how sad it all is. But I'm sure you know just how complicated he is." Kelly said, as she took the piece of cake that Grace handed to her. Grace didn't think Brendan was complicated, he was just a bigoted ass.

"I wouldn't have described him as complicated. He was pretty straight forward with his behavior. Especially toward my brother." Grace said, popping a bite of her apple cider cake into her mouth. Brendan being nothing but a pompous ass to everyone and so awful to anyone who was different. It hadn't been just Kevin that his cruelty was dished out to, other kids who had been in the LGBTQIA+ community suffered equal behavior.

"Oh yes, I remember hearing the story about how your brother hit on him." Kelly said, and Grace practically choked on her cake.

"I'm sorry, what?" Grace said after she took a sip of tea to clear her throat. This was unbelievable to her. Kevin would never dream of having a crush on Brendan. "Wow, well that is not how I or anyone else remembers it." Grace added with a laugh. "Kevin had a massive crush on someone else. Brendan had been the one to be the aggressor towards Kevin, or anyone else who was different than him. It is very interesting how he remembers things." Grace kept her tone calm, and with a tiny hint of a laugh in her voice. She didn't want to sound accusatory at all, but it's funny how narcissists love to play the victims.

"Well, I am inclined to believe you over him. So that is a clarification I can appreciate. Although, after everything I had to put up with from Brendan, I'm just surprised he just hasn't come out of the closet already. I mean, how many times can you find your husband wearing your underwear or catch him on his phone watching gay porn and not think something is up, right?" Kelly laughed, as she took another sip of her tea.

Grace just stood there in utter shock. *Brendan Moser... THE Brendan Moser... gay? Not just possibly gay, but wearing women's underwear? This wasn't possible.* It was possible that you could be straight or bisexual and enjoy watching people of the same sex having sex. Right? And it wasn't unheard of for straight men who enjoyed wearing women's clothes under their own just to feel like themselves. There was no shame in that. People should be free to do whatever they liked as long as it wasn't illegal. But having known how Brendan was in school and how he reacted towards Kevin, it made her start to question things.

"Yeah, I, uh." Grace was still trying to process everything. Kelly blushed and fiddled with the handle of her mug.

"I'm sorry, I hadn't told anyone that, I just -" Kelly's forehead creased in concern. "I don't know why but I feel very comfortable with you. I hope I didn't make you uneasy." Her gaze dropped down to her cup. Grace watched the woman retreat into herself, taking a deep breath in. She reached across the counter and took Kelly's hand.

"Hey, sorry. You have nothing to worry about. It was just surprising to hear all of that based on how he portrays himself to everyone. Your secret is safe with me." Grace squeezed Kelly's hand, allowing her to know she had nothing to fear. Exhaling a breath she was holding in, Kelly smiled back, and Grace knew then that there was more to Brendan than what meets the eye and she couldn't wait for his armor to crack.

CHAPTER TWELVE

George

School patrol was always one part nerve-wracking and one part magical. The kids always made sure to wish him a great day and talk to him, but making sure people adhered to the speed limit was a bit of a pain on any regular day. However, on days like Halloween, it was a little more difficult because of all the class parents who were having to come at multiple times of the day to pick up their kids for costume changes and then all the party supplies for the classrooms. Which delivery person was dropping off pizza versus a parent who was unloading a carload of balloons for their class party.

George wasn't sure if schools in other towns had parents like these, but Toselle Park parents went all out on their kids' class parties. As Grace's car pulled up in front of the school, Jim popped out of the passenger side door dressed as *Gomez Addams* and walked over to the trunk. George laughed at himself as tiny Grace got out of the car decked out in a *Morticia Addams* costume and long black wig. The two of them standing there looked like the complete opposite of what the characters should look like in height difference.

"Don't you two look cute? Please tell me Colin is Pugsley." George asked as he grabbed a container of cupcakes out of the trunk and started walking with Jim up to the front door. Jim rolled his eyes and just shook his head.

"Oh, he is. The whole family is the Addams Family. Grace is Morticia, Colin is Pugsley, Vivian is Wednesday, Calvin is Lurch, and Katie is Grandmama." Jim said, struggling to carry four boxes of pizza to the front door. George just laughed. He knew Grace loved Halloween, but he was just shocked they all went along with this.

"So do you have a Fester or Cousin It?" George was praying it would be someone good.

"Janie and Ken are going along with this whole thing. I completely forgot how much Grace loved dressing up. We didn't get to do this last year because she was still recouping so -" Jim started as Grace walked up with two big bags filled with goody bags and what looked like a blown-up witch's hat.

"Oh Mon Cheri, you know I love to torture you." Grace said in her best *Morticia Addams* voice as she tilted her head up for a kiss from Jim. George couldn't help but feel his heart swell for his two friends. Whether they realized it or not, theirs was a love story he had enjoyed watching unfold before his eyes. But not as much as his own.

When they returned from the cabin, George and Kevin fell right back into their lives only this time, it was filled with more love. Sexually they were taking their time. Kevin had been very understanding as it was still an adjustment for him. Being intimate with a man versus a woman seemed to be quite the adjustment. There was the difference in facial hair, and he now understood why some women didn't care for it. He preferred a clean-shaven face, which Kevin was very good about keeping up, but then there were moments at the end of the day, he didn't mind it. It reminded George that he was with the one he truly wanted to be with, five o'clock shadow and all.

The only thing that changed was that Kevin wanted to buy the cabin and then asked him to retire so that they could move up there. Shock was a complete understatement. Even though the thought had crossed his mind back when he was laid up the year before, the idea of actually retiring felt somewhat off to George. He enjoyed working, his job was so much a part of him. Yet, the hours were starting to grate on him. He had been on the force for twenty-two years, and based on his years of service, it was possible. But to move away from all his friends and family seemed wrong to him. Toselle Park had been his home for his whole life. To think about leaving that all behind was just not something he envisioned for his future.

"Can I ask you guys something?" George said, placing the cupcakes down next to Grace's bag.

"As long as you take two of these pizzas or at least place them down on the ground so my arms can get feeling back in them." Jim said. Helping him with them, George turned to the couple in front of him. They were so happy all the time. He couldn't imagine these two not being constantly in love with each other.

"Do you guys fight? Or at least not see eye to eye on stuff? You just seem like everything is perfect all the time." George asked. Jim and Grace looked at each other and began hysterically laughing.

"This one? You think I go along with every insane thing she comes up with?" Jim shook his head as Grace pouted.

"Hey, not everything I come up with is insane." George caught the glances between the two of them. Grace clearly feeling like her ideas were brilliant and Jim's quizzical glare made her roll her eyes at him. "Of course we fight, but it's not a fight per se." Grace said, smacking Jim on the arm right before hugging him. "Listen, not every relationship is the same. You just have to know your audience. Jim is easy for me to talk to, so asking him for things doesn't make me feel embarrassed or make me feel like the immediate answer is going to be a 'no'." Grace explained. "The key with the two of us is always to be open with one another. I don't hide anything from him and he doesn't hide anything from me. Yes we may not agree on stuff and we may get mad." Grace went on only to be interrupted by Jim.

"When do I make you mad?" Jim asked as Grace rolled her eyes again, prompting another snicker out of George.

"But. I take time, process my feelings and then go and talk to him once I'm calm. You catch more flies with honey than with vinegar." Grace must have had an inkling about how George was feeling about the possible move.

"Hold on, you still haven't answered me. When do I make you mad?" Jim asked again, causing a glare from Grace that George was afraid of getting.

"Right now. It was a *'for instance'* example." Grace huffed, as she looked over at George's face. "You don't want to move do you?" *Man, she is good*, George thought.

"Not particularly, but I get it. It means something to the two of us and I know he doesn't want to see me get hurt or stressed about work. But he is just as bad. He has been taking on more and more projects to build up his savings so we could both just retire early." George explained, and Grace made a cooing sound at the sweetness of the whole situation.

"Well, I think you two should talk about it a little more. We did that about our house. Actively having a good conversation is a major key to a successful partnership." Grace was right.

As the doors to the school opened, he helped Jim with the pizzas and cupcakes before heading back to his post needing to direct other parents with their cars.

They were right, he needed to talk to Kevin before anything went further. But not until after Halloween. A Friday night Halloween was going to be insane this year and he could only imagine the types of calls they were going to get.

Basher Avenue this year marked the biggest turnout they had seen due to the weather. 2024's weather was warm and most people ran out of candy early, so the trick or treating had died down a bit early. But with the cooler temperature this year, most people had no problem milling around at more of a leisurely pace, and the town preparing for the worst collected extra candy for the houses to pass out so that they wouldn't have a repeat of the year before. After dropping off candy at the Cartinos, George was on candy duty for the police department, which he always loved doing.

He had seen all his friends and family over the course of several hours and even Kevin stopped by before he went home to change into his costume for karaoke at The Sun Porch, which was set to start around seven p.m. Promising Grace that he would stop by before he officially went on patrol, George knew she would have a full plate of food ready for him.

Part of him wished that he could enjoy Halloween, especially since he always worked it. Perhaps there was something to Kevin wanting him to retire. He hadn't enjoyed a Halloween or even most holidays for years because he always volunteered to work allowing his fellow officers with families to enjoy the day with them.

As the early darkness of the night started to creep up onto the revelry, George passed off the treat duties to Tony Masuci, one of his fellow officers on the force.

"You gonna go take your dinner?" Tony asked, grabbing another box of glow sticks out of the trunk of the large police truck.

"Yeah, I'm heading over to Grace's now. I'm sure if you popped your head in she would feed you too." George mentioned. Kevin had told him to let everyone working know that if they were hungry and wanted to stop by Grace's during their rounds, they would be fed.

"Thanks. I only have another hour and then I'll be heading home. Our block is having a party so I'm gonna head there. But let

Kevin know I said thanks." Tony smiled at the little boy dressed like a dinosaur and the zombie princess next to him. George snapped his head up at the comment.

"The invite was from Grace -" he started, but Tony shot him a glare and quieted him immediately.

"Listen, I've known you my whole life and I've known Kev just as long. And we have all been waiting for the two of you to wake up. I'm just happy that you can finally be together. The gang had a bet going since last year as to how long it was gonna take. Chief won. I owe him two fifty because we all kept upping the bet." Tony grimaced, then turned to another set of kids with a smile and kept passing out glow sticks.

George couldn't believe this. The whole department sat waiting for years for this to happen. But why hadn't anyone ever said anything? Shaking his head in annoyance, George couldn't believe that everyone noticed something but didn't take the time to talk to him about it.

"One of you could have clued me in." George smirked. Tony gave him a disapproving glance.

"Would you've listened? Because I know the answer to that – Fat chance. You would have blown us off and this all would've probably taken longer." Tony laughed. He wasn't wrong. George was never one to listen to dating advice and that was the honest truth. He needed to come to these feelings on his own and in his own time. George just wished that it hadn't taken him this long.

"Fair." George admitted, as he glanced down to his watch and realized that he needed to grab something to eat before it was too late. Bidding his goodbyes to Tony, and heading through the crowd, he noticed an all too familiar face and was trying his best to avoid him. Jonathan was all dressed up as *Carmen Miranda,* stationed at a table handing out candy. The town had asked local businesses to hand out goodies and apparently his salon was there.

"Jonathan, Happy Halloween. Hope you are well." George said, as he made his way to his car. Sadly, the only way to get to it was to pass by his table. The glare that he was met with could melt a million suns, as Jonathan sneered at him.

"Well, I was having a good day till your bitchy-self showed up. Why don't you go ruin someone else's relationship… or are you just trying to ruin mine?" Jonathan said and then quickly flashed a sweet fake smile to the kids who appeared at the table for trick or treats. Taking in a deep breath to keep from saying something he was afraid to, George just smiled at Jonathan.

"Happy Halloween Jonathan. Stay safe." George said, as he walked past him only to bump directly into Brendan Moser, whose arms were full of bags of more candy. *From one hot mess to another,* George thought.

"Watch where you are going!" Brendan's tone was dripping with disdain as he shot a look past George. Glancing over his shoulder, Jonathan's eyes narrowed toward him and then turned away. George raised his brow and looked back to Brendan.

"Rumor has it, you and Kevin weren't really dating back when you put on your little show. Did you think I wouldn't find out?" Brendan said, a sneer spreading across his thin black lips. He was a zombie, and George thought *he hadn't needed much make-up to begin with considering he looked awful the last time he saw him.*

"I've actually been meaning to thank you." George smiled at him and Brendan's face contorted in confusion.

"What for?" Brendan asked.

"Well, that little kiss made me realize my feelings for Kevin. So, I guess I need to extend my warmest thanks to you for opening my eyes." George held out his hand and Brendan just stared down at it then back up to George's calm steady face. He felt a tiny bit of joy as he was enjoying this whole interaction.

"You're ridiculous. If you think I am gonna shake your hand, you have another thing coming." Brendan scoffed and brushed past George, heading over to Jonathan's table, placing down one bag of candy and then to another table to help them.

As the head of the recreation center walked up to Brendan with clip board in hand they began chatting. It seemed that Brendan had gotten himself a job. George knew that they needed an extra person to help with the community events, but he didn't think that Brendan would have been the best person to work with kids considering his character.

With a slight buzzing and vibration, George looked down at his watch and realized his dinner break was getting shorter and shorter and Kevin was finally at Grace's. Jogging over to his cruiser, George turned the ignition over and made his way there to grab a slice of pizza and finally get to have the best cupcakes in town.

He wasn't sure where Kevin purchased his costume from, but he was sure of only one thing: George had never been more turned on by a man in uniform before. Granted, he was sure he bought it off some kind of website for male strippers, because Kevin's Detective Sexy costume with short, tight shorts and body-hugging shirt was showing all the right muscles and parts that George was growing very accustomed to over the past month.

"Happy Halloween, are you here to arrest me for being too sexy? Because I am guilty on all charges." Kevin cooed as he stood in Grace's front door frame. "I believe you need to read me my rights before you cuff me." Kevin batted his eyes and held his hands out as if he was waiting to be hand-cuffed, then he straightened up. "Oh wait, do you read people their rights first or do you do it as you are cuffing them? I've never been arrested before." Kevin snapped back to his normal self. George walked up to him and kissed him on the lips, earning a sigh from him as he enveloped him in his arms.

"You need to wear this costume Sunday." George whispered, and Kevin shivered in his arms. "Because as of Sunday, I'm off for two days. I don't want to see anyone until I have to go in to work on Tuesday." Kevin's eyes widened at the prospect of the two of them possibly… finally… going to take it to the next step.

"Oh! So, you are ready, ready?" Kevin squeaked. "Because I can be all set for Sunday evening." His eyes were wild with joy and George's heart melted but fluttered with the idea that they would finally be moving forward physically. George's stomach grumbled, and as much as he wanted to stay there with Kevin in his arms, he desperately needed to eat.

"Alright, one more kiss and then I need to eat. I have only twenty minutes left before I have to get back on the road." George brushed his nose against Kevin's and kissed him one last time before heading into the house.

Grace had truly out done herself. There were realistic-looking cobwebs everywhere and the lights were changed out for flickering light bulbs, giving the rooms an eerie hue with the fire in the fireplace raging it definitely gave the whole haunted house vibes.

Kevin had told him about Grace's tendency to go all out when decorating the house. What George hadn't envisioned was just how much food would be there. He knew there would be pizza, but Grace truly was a marvel when it came to entertaining. The dining room table was covered in pizzas, a Halloween themed charcuterie board, a 'blood' punch with a floating ice brain, deviled eggs dyed purple and green making them look like rotten eggs. It boggled his mind at just how much food there was. But then he looked around the house and realized that this wasn't just some tiny party for kids. Grace it seemed invited everyone she knew.

It wasn't just the McCarren's, Gagnon's and Hank, but a bunch of other families as well. But the surprise of all people he hadn't expected to see was his own parents chatting away with Mrs. Locke and the Cartinos. He just saw them yesterday and they must have forgotten to mention they would be attending. As he grabbed a slice of pizza and shoved it in his mouth, his mother caught his eye, smiling widely at the joy of seeing him. This was everything to him. A moment that he never thought he would have. Everyone he cared about besides his sisters and their families all under one roof celebrating together. After all these years, to have so many friends and family together meant the world to him, making his heart swell and beat just a little faster than normal.

"I was not sure we would see you this evening!" She said, as he ducked just in time to miss the point of the tip of her witches hat.

"Well, if you had told me you were here, I would have come here sooner. I thought you were passing out candy?" George said, slightly garbled by the rest of the slice he was trying desperately to eat before having to leave so soon.

"How can I talk to you when you race into my house to use the restroom and then race out to go to a call? Hm?" Doreen asked, her tiny accent coming through. Mrs. Locke just laughed and shook her head at him.

"Always running. I was surprised you weren't on the track team with the way you are now." Mrs. Locke commented as she sipped her blood punch. A wise smile spread across her lips. Anytime he and Jim decided to run around the neighborhood they always stopped past her house just to say hi.

"Yeah, well I am too bulky for track, always was. Well, I have to shove more food down my throat before I head back out." George nodded graciously over to the elders in the house and shoved one more slice of pizza in his mouth before realizing he forgot something. Turning back around he looked at Ken and motioned for him to come over by him. Thankfully Ken noticed and walked over to George.

"What's up? Everything okay – Kevin isn't driving you nuts yet, is he?" Ken asked, a slight concern knitting into his brow. George smiled and shook his head.

"No actually, there is a small favor I need to ask you." George whispered, as he wrapped his arm around the older man's shoulder and brought him out into the kitchen for some peace and quiet.

It was almost midnight and all of the trick or treaters were finally all home. However, with local restaurants and groups still partying, George's only call for the evening was to one event to break up a fight. Wanting to make an appearance at Kevin's karaoke, George made his way to The Sun Porch. Making sure not to be rude, he stopped to say hi to a few of the townspeople hanging outside before heading in.

As he opened the door, he found the whole bar area was wall to wall with people. George smiled at himself. Kevin had a really great following here for his karaoke events that, if they moved away, he would have to start all over again. But he was so Hell bent on moving, knowing Kevin, George was sure that he could totally find his niche up in the Poconos. The sea of party goers were a bit overwhelming and add to it that they were all dressed in different costumes, he was having a hard time spotting Kevin.

Working his way through the crowd, he waved at a few friends and neighbors scanning the perimeter and even within the crowd to see if anyone else was wearing a fake police costume. He saw plenty of zombies, firemen, numerous superheroes, babies, witches and many more, but not a police officer in the crowd. Elbow to elbow with everyone, he turned his back, looking to see if maybe Kevin was somewhere behind him. As he backed up through the crowd, someone hit his back. It felt all too familiar. As if he had been here before. As George turned, he came face to face with Kevin who just smiled with delight.

"Hi." Kevin said, and it suddenly hit George square in the chest. The crowded bar, backing up into the person of his dreams and the only thing they uttered was the simple hello... Kevin was the person in his dreams. This whole time, his entire life – there they were right next him. He felt foolish, but as his eyes washed over Kevin's loving gaze that tiny beast in his chest cheered. Lifting his hands up to his best friend's face, he pulled him close and kissed him right there in front of the crowd, which erupted in cheers.

"Hi." George smiled, his heart renewed with complete happiness. If there was any doubts about what he talked to Ken about, they all washed away at this exact moment. The person of his dreams this entire time was Kevin.

"I wasn't sure you were going to get here?" Kevin questioned, and George knew that he meant just for that night, but the truth of it was that it had taken him forever to get to this exact moment.

"I'm just glad I finally got here. I love you." George placed a sweet peck on his lips and then gazed down to the Detective Sexy badge. "And maybe to catch you in this outfit again." George winked, he did love this costume. It showed off Kevin's physique very well, and he felt himself getting just a little too turned on looking over his body. Batting his eyes at George, Kevin smiled brightly and shrugged.

"It's what I do. I look cute in everything I wear." Kevin quipped back and then looked back to the stage where the signer was finishing their song. "Okay, I love you, but I need to get to work. I'll see you when I get home." With another quick peck on his lips, Kevin winked and disappeared back into the crowd. Stopping by the bar to say hi to a few of the bartenders, George made his way back out to the parking lot ready to wrap up the rest of his night. As the cool midnight air breezed across the blush that Kevin's kisses had caused, George smiled to himself as he made his way to the cruiser. He had another hour left in his shift and he was hoping it would be a nice quiet night. That was until he recognized Jonathan's fruit-topped hat that he had been wearing standing near a car he knew for sure wasn't his. The area was not well lit making it impossible to make out who he was talking to. But whoever it was, they were in tattered clothes dressed like a zombie. Positive he saw this costume earlier, it was impossible to know for sure, especially since zombies was a very popular costume.

George hid behind the pillar, trying his best to observe as quietly and discreetly as he could, knowing full well that Jonathan viewed him as public enemy number one. But this late at night, in the dark, George's instinct was to make sure that he was okay despite everything that had transpired with Kevin. Whoever this other person was with him, didn't seem to want to harm Jonathan. As George watched the two men getting closer, Jonathan wrapped his arms around the other man's neck leaning in for a kiss. He hadn't seen Gerald earlier, so he just chalked it up to it being him. However, the frame was too wide and heavy to be Gerald. The distance was not helping him figuring it out. Reckoning that Jonathan was safe, George proceeded to his cruiser and got in.

This Halloween, despite having to work, had truly been great. And all George wanted was for time to pass quickly so he could head home and get some rest in the arms of the man of his dreams.

CHAPTER THIRTEEN

Kevin

Sitting at the kitchen island in his parents' house, Kevin's mind wandered as he played with the cream cheese he was supposed to be smearing on his bagel. George had gotten home before himself, not wanting to wake him, Kevin slipped into the bed next to him. Smiling to himself, the echoes of the soft snore from George as he laid there the night before had his mind wandering. When did his life become so perfect? The only sad part was that George was up and out the door before he woke up to the sound of his ringer going off to Grace reminding him about brunch.

He felt his father's eyes on him, snapping Kevin out of his daze.

"I was wondering if I was going to have to start waving something in front of your face to break you from your chain of thoughts. Everything okay?" Ken asked, looking back at his newspaper

– a ritual that his dad couldn't seem to break despite the availability of digital news, was actually reading a physical newspaper.

"Yeah, just happy, swimming in my feels." Kevin smiled. Ken nodded to him with a soft smile.

"Well, I'm glad both my kids are happy finally." Ken added, as Janie headed into the kitchen with a basket in her hand bustling around trying to find something.

"Ugh, the gang will be here soon and I can't find my -" Janie turned her back to them as she rummaged through a drawer and then squealed. "Ah! I found it." Waving a doily type fabric above her head. "Ugh, I don't even know why I use this thing, no one even notices." She said walking over to the island, placing the basket in an empty space and then laying the doily in the bottom before loading up all the bagels Ken had gotten from the shop that morning.

"Oh, we notice. Grace and I have already figured out which one of us will get all your stuff." Kevin said, finishing dressing his bagel. Janie's head snapped up and looked appalled.

"Whatta ya mean, you and Grace figured out who gets what? I'm not even cold and you are divvying up all my stuff! Kenny, do you hear this?" Janie barked and huffed as she kept setting up the rest of the bagels and then turned to plate the muffins. Ken just nodded to her.

"Yeah, I already know who gets what." Ken calmly said, not even raising his eyes from his newspaper. The shocked gasp from Janie caused Kevin to nearly spit out the sip of coffee he had just taken.

"Unreal! You are all rotten. I'm not even sick, or dead yet and you three – you three! You're all awful. Just don't bury me in the ground over at St. Gert's. It floods over there. Otherwise, I will be waiting with St. Peter right at the gates to yell at you all for getting water up my ass." Janie threatened, pointing a butter knife at both Kevin and Ken.

Grabbing the basket and whisking it away, Janie made her way into the hallway with another huff. Taking a bite of his bagel, Kevin looked outside to see Grace and her gaggle making their way into the house. Closing his eyes, he braced himself for the roar of commotion that was about to break the comfortable silence that he and his dad were enjoying.

"I told you not to ask her out, she's a bitch!" Katie argued, as she burst through the door with Calvin steady on her heels, red in the face.

"Yeah well, I hope you're enjoying that piece of shit you call a boyfriend! You know he is only dating you to try and get you in bed, right?" Calvin spat back. The chorus of *hey, knock it off* from the adults as they ambled into the house was almost deafening, prompting Janie to come running.

"Alright, enough both of you." Grace yelled and pointed to Calvin, "You go sit and eat." Then turning to Katie, she pointed to her stepdaughter. "You come outside with me." Jim went to make a comment until Grace shot him a look and took Katie by the hand, walking her back outside. Kevin heard the garage door open and he knew that Grace was taking Katie to cool off in the Camaro that Jim had finally finished the week before.

"I don't miss this." Ken said, still reading his paper. Janie wandered in, ushering Vivian and Colin into the dining room to eat, giving Jim the chance to sit at the island for a few seconds. Kevin saw the exhaustion on Jim's face and wondered if it was a hangover or just being tired from such a busy day before.

"So that was intense. You look like death, what's going on?" Kevin questioned. Jim just shook his head.

"They like each other. But because they are stepsister and brother they are trying to date other people thinking it is going to get each other out of their systems." Jim sighed. Kevin's heart went out to the two teens. He knew what it was like to have feelings for someone and think they could never be together. Now, being related by marriage was going to be a bit taboo, especially for a small town. The truth was, they weren't related by blood at all and if they really wanted they could date. But the simple fact that they were teens made it harder.

"Would you and Grace be okay if they did?" Kevin asked. He didn't have kids so he wasn't sure what was right and what was wrong. There was a part of him that would have loved to have kids of his own - but seeing how Grace and all his friends had to deal with different things with them, he was grateful he didn't.

"At this point, we're just trying to survive the hormones and now Vivian is starting up as well." Jim ran his hands over his face, taking a big breath in. "The thing is, I saw Cal starting to have feelings for Katie as soon as they met, but Grace is just worried that it is possible they are trauma bonding. My personal opinion? He's just a raging teenager, so pretty much every girl looks good to him." Jim explained, sipping the coffee he had made while chatting with them. Kevin couldn't tell, but it seemed that Jim had a little soft spot for Calvin.

Shaking her head as she entered the room, Janie gave Jim a slight squeeze on his shoulder before grabbing the large bottle of orange juice off the counter.

"Ugh, I do not envy you and Grace, he is in a fit to be tied. How long has he been this way?" Janie asked. It seemed that Calvin wasn't hangry, he was just being a grump. Figuring he knew what it was like to have a crush on someone for so long and the feeling of wanting the unattainable – Kevin thought he would take a shot at talking to the teen.

Allowing Jim and his parents to talk, Kevin walked into the dining room to a vexed Calvin and two rather cautious-looking siblings sitting at the table. Smiling to them, he slid into the chair across from Calvin and wrapped his arm around Colin.

"Mind if I join you?" Kevin chirped. Colin and Vivian looked relieved to have someone other than their older brother in the room with them, as Calvin barely even acknowledged that he was at the table. Glancing over at Calvin, who had piled up so much food on his plate, Kevin thought it was a good thing he was so young and wouldn't get heartburn as he shoveled scrambled eggs into his mouth.

"So, get any good candy I can come over and steal? I didn't get to go trick or treating." Kevin laughed as Calvin grumbled incoherently to himself.

"Get your own." Calvin spat, and Kevin arched his brow. This was not his normal happy nephew. Grinning down to Vivian and Colin, Kevin needed to stop this behavior. "Listen, why don't you go check with Grammie Janie and see if she needs any help." The two younger kids practically ran from the room as Calvin just kept stuffing his face.

"Whoever, the Hell you are, you need to leave and bring my nephew back. Because you are acting like a dick." Kevin's voice dropped and returned his nephew's attitude right back at him. He normally only reserved this for the worst of people. However, the human sitting across from him wasn't anyone he felt like he knew.

"That's fucked up, is that what you say to your oldest nephew?" Calvin garbled with a bite of bagel in his mouth.

"Listen, you little shit! I wiped your ass, so watch the language. Just because some chick didn't want to go out with you, doesn't mean you get to punish us!" Kevin snapped back. He wasn't going to take it from Calvin no matter how upset he was. And if there was anyone who understood what he was going through, it was him. Calvin looked up from his plate, and his eyes said it all. His sadness and desperation shone through and Kevin's heart sank for him as he watched Calvin's eyes glaze over. Getting up from his seat, Kevin walked over and wrapped his arms around Calvin, allowing him to finally break down.

Kevin knew his nephew was going to counseling so maybe this wasn't just about teenage heartbreak. Hearing footsteps in the hallway, Kevin motioned with his hand to whoever was coming to leave. Calvin buried his head into Kevin's shirt, allowing the tears to fall and to take a moment for his feelings to wash over him. Kevin wasn't sure what the right length of time was to hold someone when they were so upset, but something in him knew not to let go until the other person was done.

As Calvin collected himself, he pulled away and looked up at Kevin.

"Sorry." Calvin whispered, as he wiped his nose with his sleeve and wiped his cheeks. "I knew Becca wasn't going to say yes, I just hoped that someone else would have seen me instead." Calvin sniffled.

Kevin knew just who Calvin was talking about now that Jim had given him some insight.

"Boy, do I know what that was like. Listen, just because I am your uncle, doesn't mean that I can't sit and listen. I was a teenage boy once, a million years ago." Kevin smiled at the teen, who gave him a sarcastic glare.

"You were into boys, I'm into girls. There is a difference." Calvin complained. Kevin shook his head in disagreement.

"Just because you like one sex and I like the other doesn't mean that I don't know what it feels like to have feelings for someone and them not have them back for you." Kevin explained. Looking at him with fresh eyes, Calvin took a sip of his juice and sighed. "You want to tell me about her? Anyone I know that I could help you with?" He was taking a chance that perhaps Calvin would confide in him so that at least his sister could get some clarity. But the teen was seeing right through him. With the roll of his eyes, Calvin just shook his head.

"I'm not telling you, because you will just tell Mom." Calvin said, taking another bite of his bagel.

"I can keep a secret!" Kevin threw his hands up, offended at the inference that he would betray his trust, but even as he said it, he knew he was lying.

"You keep telling yourself that, Gossip Queen. But thanks for trying. I'll be okay." Calvin said with a half-smile. Kevin pouted his lips knowing that he wasn't going to get any more out of him. Sitting in silence, Kevin looked at the teenage young man sitting next to him. He wasn't sure when he had grown up. It felt as if Grace just came home with him and was dodging streams of pee while trying to change his diapers. He enjoyed his time with them, but the fact that it had taken him this long to find his person made him realize that it was all for the best. He was the *funcle* – the fun uncle, and it was a title he would relish for his whole life.

After a lengthy pause he looked at Calvin, kissed the top of his head and said, "I'm here if you ever want to talk."

Calvin arched his brow and without a word, Kevin knew he was questioning whether he would say anything to Grace.

"And I promise, on all that I love, I will never say anything. You just need to text or call, okay?" Kevin wanted him to be okay. With a half-quirked grin Calvin nodded, Kevin just hoped that he would take him up on the offer to chat if he needed it.

As he watched the clock tick away, Kevin's excited nervousness wracked his body at the anticipation of waiting for George to get home. Trying his best not to eat for the day, he had prepped for the night and stuck with sipping on another orange juice as he tried to relax. Even though George was working, he wanted to surprise him and hoped that maybe he wouldn't be too exhausted to finally have that night he spent days dreaming about.

Glancing around the bedroom Kevin checked to make sure that everything was right where it needed to be. Candles, two different lubes, condoms, a wedge pillow and a fresh set of sheets on the bed. Kevin knew that George didn't need all the frills but considering it was going to be their first time, he just wanted to make it special. In the past, sex would sometimes be spontaneous, but Kevin absolutely hated messy sex. If he hadn't prepped beforehand, he would insist on sex in the shower, and although that wasn't out of the question for the next couple of days, he wanted tonight to be special.

Walking back into the bathroom, he put on a fresh mist of cologne, fixed his hair and then put his Detective Sexy outfit on. Checking out his own ass in the mirror to make sure it looked amazing, he then turned to make sure the whole look was perfect as he put on his hat. Smiling at himself, his heart raced and then stopped for a second when there was a tiny creak of the floorboards just outside the bathroom. George stood there smiling widely at him as Kevin tried to regain his composure after screaming at the top of his lungs.

"Oh my God, you don't make a sound do you?" Kevin squealed, fanning himself as he felt faint. George glided into the bathroom snaking his arms around Kevin's waist pulling him close.

"I'm like a cat, light on my feet." George quipped, lightly kissing Kevin's lips, stirring a fire deep in his loins. He would have taken George this second, but he wasn't about to just rush the whole night. Kevin had certain things he needed to attend to before they could have fun. The butt plug that he was using to stretch himself out in preparation for George was still in and he wasn't sure just how to explain that one to George. He hadn't needed his old training kit in years and tossed it out. However, right after they started seeing each other and exploring their bodies, Kevin ran out and bought a new one due to George's length and girth.

His body tingled at the idea of where tonight was going to go, and as if George could read his thoughts, Kevin felt his hands sliding down his lower back and over the short shorts he had on. George's large hands grasped Kevin's ass cheeks and squeezed, earning himself a moan that escaped Kevin's lips. The tips of his fingers teased the seam of Kevin's toned ass, and it took everything in him not to let George strip him right there. Delicious ripples of electricity ran through Kevin as George backed him up against the wall. Clearly, George was not tired from such a long shift, Kevin thought smiling to himself.

"What is the smile for?" George asked, pulling away from their kiss, his hands now starting to undo the buttons on the front of Kevin's costume. Fortunately, George had the good sense to take off most of his work gear before coming home, leaving him wearing his undershirt and pants. No longer willing to wait, Kevin joined George in getting him out of his work clothes.

"Because I was expecting you to say that you were too tired. I was taking a shot in the dark for tonight." Kevin said, struggling with George's buckle to free his shirt. Stilling Kevin's hands with his own, George pushed them away and then pushed Kevin harder against the wall. Kevin's ass slapped against it putting pressure on the plug, sending a charge right to Kevin's balls. His cock grew harder as he watched George's gaze darken and a smirk spread across his lips.

Backing away from him, George relaxed against the bathroom counter and slowly moved to his belt, never taking his eyes off of Kevin. Methodically unhooking his belt, he slowly pulled it from the loops on his waistband and folded it in half in his hand, devilishly smiling at Kevin.

"I've never tied someone up before with my belt, would you be interested?" George asked, hesitation in his eyes, but Kevin's head swam in a sea of ecstasy. He hadn't mentioned this before, but he actually loved a little bondage and teasing. He never would have imagined George would be interested in something like that.

"Oh, I would very much be interested in that." Kevin's eyes darkened as they trailed down to the waistband of George's pants, allowing his view to go lower and he could see just how turned on George was. Not willing to wait any longer, Kevin reached out and unbuttoned his work pants, taking his time unzipping and George's eyes never leaving his gaze. His dark brown eyes were almost black from the heightened tension building between them as Kevin slid his fingers along the seam of his boxers and lowered them, falling down to his knees to help George out of them.

George had removed his socks and shoes, which would explain how he crept around the house so quietly, but also made removing his pants so easy. Kevin's heart raced and he looked up as George took off his shirt. He was *perfection*. George was an exquisite male form. *Adonis*, Kevin thought, and he was all his. He thought about all the beautiful women and men out there in the world that George could have chosen to be with, but here in his home, he was Kevin's.

Kneeling in front of George, his face was perfectly positioned in front of the magnificent specimen of a cock that he was thinking about all day long. Reaching up, cupping his tight balls in his hand, Kevin slowly stroked George's shaft a pearl of pre-cum seeping from the crown. Not wanting to waste a single drop, Kevin licked it slowly, swirling it around the head of his dick and sucked softly, earning a throaty moan from George. Kevin had never felt so accomplished before to hear a moan, but George's he never took for granted. He was the only man George wanted, and to make him feel so comfortable meant the world to him.

As George rolled his head back enjoying Kevin's warm wet tongue licking and playing with him, he threaded his fingers through Kevin's hair and yanked his head back.

"If you keep doing that I will not want you to stop and I have other plans for us." George growled as Kevin rose from his knees and wrapped his arms around his neck. George's large hands skimmed over Kevin's back, then to his chest, continuing to unbutton the costume which Kevin needed out of this very second. Scrambling to get the shirt off, they both looked at each other and laughed as they kissed.

"Why do I feel like a fumbling teenager right now?" George asked. Kevin noticed George's hands slightly trembling as he went to the next button. Embracing his hands with his own, Kevin looked up to George with complete warmth in his eyes.

"If it makes you feel any better, I'm a bit nervous too. Fooling around is one thing, but sex is a whole other. If you still aren't rea -" Kevin was cut off by George's kiss and he exhaled all his tense feelings in one long breath.

"I'm ready, in case you didn't notice. I just don't know if I'll fit." George chuckled, but Kevin merely smiled and licked the tip of his nose.

"I told you; I have been preparing for you. Everything will be fine. But I do need a private moment to take care of something. I will meet you in the bedroom, everything is all set up." Kevin said before kissing away the curious look on George's face. Pulling away from his warm body was difficult, but he had needed him out of the bathroom and in bed.

CHAPTER FOURTEEN

George

He wasn't going to argue with a determined Kevin, and being just a bit curious, he wanted to see just what Kevin had done in the bedroom. Gathering his clothes from the floor, he gave a quick peck to Kevin's lips before heading out into the hallway and into their room. His bedroom somehow became theirs over the past month. It was little, tiny touches that Kevin placed throughout George's room that made it theirs. Kevin was the color against his drab gray backdrop. He had added plants and an air filter in the room that produced amazing effects on George's sleep. However, the room he entered was something utterly remarkable.

The pumpkin-colored sheets on their bed and the sharp pop of color against his white and gray comforter was actually brilliant. The candles throughout gave a soft amber glow and made the room almost ethereal. To someone else's eye, it was just a bedroom made for sex, but not for George. This was calculated, precise and perfect. For someone like George who was used to routine and very rarely operated outside of it, he appreciated that Kevin had put so much time and effort into making their first time so special.

Most men wouldn't make a big deal over their partner setting the mood. The mass majority of the time it really wasn't for them; it was more for women. But this gesture, the sweet thought and sentimentality that went behind this made his heart skip a beat. This moment right here, he knew for sure that nothing and no one had ever made him feel this way before. George knew he loved Kevin - he told him so after all these years. And even though they confessed their feelings early on, he knew for sure that he never wanted to be with anyone else.

Tossing his clothes into the hamper, he charged over to his dresser and opened his sock drawer, pulling out the velvet bag he had hidden all the way in the back. Opening the bag and tipping the contents out into his hand, George smiled and turned to the door, checking to see if Kevin was there yet. He hadn't thought of what to say. He told Ken what his plan for Christmas Eve was going to be and received his blessing. But deep in his bones he knew tonight was much more than what was going to happen in this room.

Kevin was his home. Not the building, not the rooms – it was him. His heart now stammering against his ribs as he waited for Kevin. He wasn't sure if he should be standing or not. Hearing the bathroom door open, George dropped to his knee and held up the item in his hand. Kevin had put on his robe and stopped short in the doorway as he caught the sight of George on his knee holding out a ring.

"Oh my God! Wait! What?" Kevin choked, as his eyes glazed over and brimming with tears. George's own vision started to blur and burn from the tears that were threatening to escape.

"Kevin, no one has meant more to me in my entire life. To have fallen in love with my friend is great, but with my best friend makes it so much more. You are all the more I could ask for in my life. Every time I have had my heart broken, you were there. When my parents were sick, you were there. Because you weren't just my friend, you were my partner before I could even say you were. And to have someone so loving and caring, someone to hold my hand in the darkest times, I couldn't have asked for a better person by my side. So now I ask you if you would be mine. Be that person by my side for the rest of my life." George asked, a tear rolling down his cheek. Kevin inched his way closer, the tears and choked back sobs coming from his throat were all the answer George needed. Rising to his feet, he reached out and took Kevin's hand into his and slid the ring onto Kevin's ring finger as he nodded his head wildly over and over again.

George couldn't believe it. He accomplished the impossible – he had finally gotten Kevin to shut up. A sly grin spread across his lips as he gathered Kevin into his arms and kissed him reverently at first. Kevin's lips were soft and inviting. He was to be his. The joy coursing through George's veins that he was finally getting his happily ever after was something new to him. He assumed that he would just be a confirmed old bachelor for his whole life, but now with Kevin at his side he would never be alone.

Deepening his kiss, George held Kevin as if he would float away or disappear forever. He needed him - mind, body and soul. Wanting to fuse himself to Kevin, his body ached as he could feel his body reacting to him. The lean form against his urged him for more. Kevin was to be his and he would make sure he would know that there was no one else in this world beyond him.

Sucking on Kevin's bottom lip, George started trailing kisses down to his chin, along Kevin's jaw line and to his ear. Remembering that Kevin loved it a little rough, George first made soft tiny caresses on his earlobe, then skimmed his tongue along the lower edge, and then finally took it into his mouth to take a quick nip and sucked down hard before releasing it. Shuddering in his arms, he felt Kevin's hardened cock twitch at the sensation, causing George to smile to himself. He loved that he turned Kevin on as much as he did.

"Get the belt." George whispered, a tiny squeak escaping Kevin's lips as he stilled in his arms.

"Yes sir." Kevin choked out as he tried to compose himself long enough to pull away from George's strong grip and run to the dresser where George had left it. The glee in Kevin's eyes were palpable enough to fill the whole room, *but that was Kevin*, George thought to himself. His light, his color in his normally black and white world. Giggling to himself, Kevin returned with the belt, his smile wider than the universe and George's heart swelled so much it felt as if it would burst right out of his body.

Quickly tossing off the robe onto the floor, Kevin handed George the belt. As he slowly wrapped the belt around his fist, George slid his fingers through Kevin's hair then tightened his grip on the back of his head and pulled him in. Crushing his lips onto Kevin's this time with the heat of a thousand suns exploding around him. George's blood pulsed throughout his whole body as he backed Kevin up to the bed.

"I've never done this before, so you are going to have to let me know just how soft or hard you want this." George stated. He was inexperienced in everything they were about to do, but if there was anyone who would be willing to guide him through this experience – it was Kevin. There were years of friendship and trust between them. And George knew he would never want to hurt him in any way, unless Kevin wanted it.

"Oh, I will definitely let you know. My safe word is pineapple. If it becomes too much I will say that." Kevin's eyes were smokey with lust as he bit his lip, but George was slightly taken aback.

"You have a safe word? So, you've done this before?" George asked. Kevin's expression changed from devilish to apprehensive in a flash.

"Once – twice – okay a couple of times. I like being tied up and my hair pulled – and before you say anything, girls don't get to corner the market on liking getting their hair pulled, okay?" Kevin snipped, but George couldn't help but snicker just a little as he threw the belt onto the bed and went back to lacing his fingers into Kevin's hair. His soft black waves curling around George's fingers, he did love when he could gather a bunch of it into his hand and pull. He had learned over the past month that Kevin loved that and actually let his hair grow out just a little so he had more to grab.

Taking a fist full of the hair at the nape of Kevin's head, George pulled his head back and started kissing down Kevin's neck. Melting right there in George's arm, Kevin moaned as George slid his other hand over his body, his fingers finding all the ridges of muscle that Kevin worked so hard to build. The pads of George's fingers left goose-prickled skin in their wake as he finally found purchase and squeezed hard onto Kevin's ass again.

Excitement rolled over him in waves at the idea of Kevin bent over, moaning his name over and over again… No longer willing to wait, George whirled Kevin around and started kissing Kevin's long neck resting his hands on his hips. Fingers curling into the soft flesh of Kevin's hips, George ground himself against his ass sending jolts of fiery electricity running through his whole body.

Coaxing Kevin to bend over with his hands behind his back, George took the belt off the bed and began latching the belt around Kevin's wrists. A deep heat swirled in his chest as the beast deep inside of him growled at the sight of Kevin easily submitting to him. He found himself suddenly having the urge to slap his ass. Without warning George reached back and slapped Kevin hard on his right ass cheek leaving a stinging residue in his own hand. A yelp escaped Kevin's mouth and then a low growl George had never heard before.

"Again." Kevin begged, his breath catching in the back of his throat. The creature in George's soul darkened his eyes as he looked down at the red handprint on Kevin's right cheek. Shifting over just an inch, George thought that the left one needed a twin. As he reached back again he slapped that one, the muscles vibrating under his palm as Kevin stuttered out a strangled moan.

"God, fuck me now." Kevin pleaded, muffling the sounds of his mews into the pillow his head was resting on. Without hesitation, George grabbed the lube off of the nightstand and started stroking himself. The lube was cool at first and then warmed as he stroked his shaft over and over. He wanted to make sure Kevin was as comfortable as he could be, so he put a little more onto his thumb, reached down and swirled it around Kevin's waxed hole. Sighing into the pillow, Kevin pushed himself into George, begging for more, and more was what he was going to get.

Lining himself up, George eased the crown of his dick slowly into Kevin and immediately felt him tighten around him as a whimper escaped into the pillow Kevin was biting.

"Are you -" George started asking but quickly stopped as Kevin just shook his head.

"I'm not saying the word, keep going." Kevin mumbled. Gathering up Kevin's bound hands, George felt Kevin relax around him and finally pushed further. The stretch of Kevin's ass around his engorged cock was impressive as it clinched around him. Women felt one way, but this was unbelievably different. Not a bad different, just different.

Pulling Kevin up to a standing position, he drove home as deep as he could. The collective grunting from them both drove that little beast in George's chest to start moving. It wanted more; it needed more. As George rhythmically thrust slowly into Kevin, the gasps and moans egged on this hidden side of him. His one hand was on Kevin's hip, and the other had released Kevin's bound hands and moved around to find the thing he wanted to hold.

Kevin's cock was only semi-hard, probably due to the pressure that he was causing, but if he was going to cum, so was Kevin. As his best friend's head landed on his shoulder, George grasped Kevin's long shaft in his hand, bending his head to kiss him again as he stroked him. Slow at first, matching in time with his own speed, swallowing whines and gasps, until he wasn't sure he liked the fact that Kevin couldn't touch him.

George needed Kevin's hands on his skin, to feel his nails raking against his muscles never wanting to let go. Releasing Kevin's dick, George went to work on unlatching the belt.

"I'm sorry but you need to touch me." George grunted as he thrust hard into Kevin, the slapping of the bodies coming together, echoing in the room mingling with Kevin's high-pitched moans. With Kevin's hands finally released, George's mind swirled the moment Kevin grasped his ass pulling him closer, guiding him into a pace they would both get to enjoy. Their bodies were hot and sweaty as George continued thrusting and stroking Kevin as he started to feel the building release, the tingle in his spine and his balls tightening.

"Harder" Kevin begged in between kisses. George's thrusts became more erratic as he pumped Kevin's weeping cock, and just when he couldn't take it anymore, his body fell over the cliff. His own climax came just as Kevin's did, and streams of cum fell from his fiancé's dick onto the pillow he had been biting earlier. With ragged breaths and breathy sighs, the two of them held each other tight in their embrace. George was complete as long as he was with Kevin.

His magical dream of Kevin yelling his name was interrupted by the insistent knocking on the front door. Still snoring in his arms, Kevin didn't even stir, blissfully unaware of the knocking that didn't want to stop or the dinging of his phone next to the bed that was sounding off with persistent text messages. Kissing the top of Kevin's head, George slowly pulled his arm out from under Kevin and grabbed a pair of lounge pants out of his dresser. Whoever was bothering them, had better have a good reason.

He could tell that whoever was standing on the other side of the door was a woman based on the tone of the knock. Most men are heavy handed, while women are quick and repetitive.

"You have got to be kidding me." Nikki's voice muffled through the door. George's shoulders dropped, releasing the tension of what could have been an emergency, but knowing that it was Nikki on the other side, he knew this was just about gossip. Opening the door, he found the petite blonde standing there looking down at her phone with a scowl on her face.

"Well, it's about time! I've been knocking for twenty minutes. Where is Kevin?" Nikki demanded, as she barged her way through the doorway. George just stood there stunned, not quite sure how to respond to her.

"Um, good morning to you as well. Please come in." George snarked back as Nikki made herself comfortable on the couch. A shuffling noise from the back hallway brought George's attention to Kevin who was standing there rubbing his eyes, his morning wood tenting his low hanging lounge pants as he fixed his glasses.

"Who the fu -" Kevin started, as his eyes then focused on Nikki. "Girl, what part of two-day sex-a-thon did you miss? Nothing is more important than me getting head and dick." Kevin explained with his hands on his hips, knowing full well George was still standing right there. The warmth spreading across George's face caught him off guard. He knew that Kevin would have talked to Nikki, they were best friends, but George hadn't expected him to be so blunt with her right in front of him.

Not sure what to do with himself, George started making his way to the kitchen.

"I'm just going to put on a pot of coffee; I will let the two of you chat." George placed a tiny peck on Kevin's cheek as he made his way into the kitchen.

The clock on the stove read ten forty-five a.m. and he blinked twice, because he had never slept so peacefully or this late in his entire life. Rubbing his face with his hands trying to wake up, George started to make a fresh pot of coffee. As he filled the coffee pot with water, he could make out muffled words coming from Nikki and Kevin's conversation in the living room. *No way are you sure; absolutely not;* and *give me a break* were the only phrases he could hear over the sound of the water.

Nikki must have either heard or seen something and, to no surprise, couldn't wait to tell Kevin. This was their thing - one of them heard something and then desperately needed to tell the other. George was not one for gossip, in fact it annoyed him at times that Kevin was so enthralled with hearing it, but after all these years, George wasn't about to change him.

"Hold on, I'm just finding this all so difficult to believe. Brendan hates gay men. Is she sure she saw him at the salon? I can't imagine him going to Jonathan for a haircut, let alone working for him." Kevin questioned. The idea that Brendan was working at the salon took George by surprise as well. He recalled Brendan and Safar talking on Halloween and he had assumed that Brendan was working at the recreation center, but that apparently wasn't the case. His instincts had been thrown off. Usually, he was really good at reading people and gestures, but for the first time he must have been wrong.

As the pot sputtered the last of the coffee into the pot, George poured three mugs and brought it out on a tray he grabbed from the cupboard with the cream and sugar. Clearing his throat, he placed the tray down on the dining room table. Kevin, smelling the delicious aroma, pulled his head away from Nikki's attention and got up from his spot. If there was anything that could pull Kevin away from gossip, it was a freshly brewed cup of coffee.

Walking up to George, Kevin just smiled, placing a warm kiss on his lips. It was tiny and simple, but it was in these moments that George knew he was thankful that Kevin agreed to be his. And then the thought hit him. No one knew yet. Nikki was sitting right there, and Kevin hadn't said a single word about it. George didn't care about gossip, he cared about truth and this was the biggest piece of news that he could share.

"Nikki, there is coffee here, if you would like a cup to go with your congratulations we haven't gotten yet." George said. Kevin's head snapped up and realized exactly what he meant. Joy gleamed in his eyes as he covered his mouth with his left hand, and George smiled as Kevin squealed.

Nikki's head was down looking at her phone going through text messages.

"Yeah congrats on finally having sex, that only took forever." Nikki's unamused tone hit Kevin right in the chest, spurning him to turn and give her the *ahem* sound. George watched as Nikki looked up and her face went from total annoyance to utter shock.

"No fucking way! No fucking way! Are you kidding me? You're engaged?" Nikki screamed. George's ears were now ringing from the deafening shrieks coming from both her and Kevin. He knew that this would possibly be the response. Their friends and families would be thrilled, but after last night there was no chance he would wait until Christmas Eve. It had been perfection. How could he not propose after Kevin had taken so much time and effort to make last night magical for them both?

"We haven't told the families yet, so hand over the phone so we can call them and tell them ourselves and not hear it through the grapevine." George said, holding out his hand, waiting for Nikki to release her phone. A dejected pout bloomed across her lips, but she hesitantly handed him her phone, acquiescing to his request.

"Can I at least be here when you call them? I am just so thrilled I got to be the first to find out, but I want to hear what they have to say." She asked. Nikki sounded just like Mandy, but maybe it was that Mandy sounded like her. Mothers and daughters have that way about themselves and mimic each other's behaviors.

Exchanging glances with Kevin, who was still showing off the simple white gold band with a few inset diamonds, George shook his head and reached for his own phone that he had left on the table the night before. Dialing up his own parents first, they told them of the joyous news. George's parents always supportive of his life so far, it was no wonder the second he finally realized his feelings for Kevin that they would be thrilled for him. He had seen just how amazing they could be. Sincere happiness for their child and the life he would build with his partner was their deepest wish for him, to be happy forever no matter what gender his person would be.

Overjoyed at the news, Dorren instantly decided that they would be inviting the Cartinos' whole family over to celebrate Thanksgiving together. Which meant another nine people they would be trying to cram into their home. With his whole family plus them it would be twenty-five people in their home, but Doreen was beyond insistent that she would make it work.

Their next call was to Kevin's parents. Calling Ken's phone, they waited for him to answer.

"Ever since Grace got married he barely carries his phone. We should have called Mom instead." Kevin said. Before he took the phone to hang up, a soft breathy male voice answered the line.

"Hey Kev, everything okay?" Ken said, sounding slightly out of breath.

"Yeah, I'm fine. Why are you out of breath?" Kevin asked, his concerned gaze hitting George square in the chest. His dad would go walking to keep healthy with his heart condition but it almost sounded like he was whispering, and considering the time, even George couldn't figure out why he would be speaking so low.

"Well, my phone was in the kitchen and your mother was yelling at me in front of Judi and Mark to go get it. I saw it was you and I am trying to save you from having to talk to her." Ken explained. George laughed inwardly, Ken knew his wife far too well, he thought.

"Well, unfortunately, you need to get her, because I need to speak to both of you." Kevin was practically giggling as he said this. George's chest swelled with the joy that Kevin was emitting. He already knew that Ken was going to be elated even though the timeline had changed. Practically crushing his ribs with the hug, he gave him after giving his blessing, George knew Ken would be glad he didn't have to keep this secret any longer from Janie.

The muffled sound of Ken's hand brushing against the mic of the phone scratched hard and they could hear the murmurs of Janie and Judi's voices in the background.

"Kevin's on the phone; he needs to talk to us." Ken said, the echoing sound of being on speakerphone made it clear that he was going to share the conversation with everyone else there. George's gaze went from the phone to Kevin's glowing face. His eyes were glassy as tears brimmed at the surface and he took in a staggered breath before he spoke.

"I'm getting married." Kevin choked out as the tears rolled down his cheeks. It was that moment that truly made it feel like it was real. George knew that there would be no more days of feeling lonely, of feeling like something was missing. He had it all right there under his nose his whole life. The ache in George's cheeks from the smile that spread from ear to ear as Kevin and Nikki chatted with Janie on the other end of the phone was something he could get accustomed to. This was the happiest he had ever seen Kevin, and that warmth, that love was all he would ever need for the rest of his life.

CHAPTER FIFTEEN

Grace

Time appeared to fly since George and Kevin announced their engagement. Sadly, despite the good news, Grace was still no closer to finally settling on a story she was happy with. Putting her current work in progress on hold, she sat in her office crocheting what she was hoping would be a blanket. A quiet knock on the door stopped her concentration and she silently prayed it wasn't Kevin again.

As much as she loved her brother and was thrilled beyond words that they were getting married, he had made it a daily habit to come over and ask her a bunch of questions about what he should do about the wedding. That wasn't the part that she minded. It was the fact that they still hadn't picked a date, and for someone like Grace that needs all her ducks in a row, it irritated the Hell out of her. Her eyes burned, as she blinked trying to refocus her vision. Taking in a deep calming breath, she braced for Kevin's bridezilla complex to come charging through her door and she resigned herself to a long painful discussion.

"Come in." Grace said, a quiet hesitation in her voice. As she braced for Kevin, her whole body miraculously eased the second Denise opened the door. Thankfully, she was not a bridezilla.

"Girl!" Denise uttered, her eyes wide and filled with mischief. Practically falling off her chair, Grace matched Denise's grin knowing she had gossip and it was gonna be good. "I'm not interrupting, cause I can come back." Denise teased standing at the door, glancing from the yarn and then to Grace's laptop.

"Bitch, you don't stop my ass from writing with that *Girl!* shit." Grace didn't know who she was lying to, Denise or herself. Denise's brow raised at the cold laptop and then back to Grace.

"You weren't writing, you were crocheting." Denise giggled. Grace knew she couldn't even deny it with the beginning of her pink and green blanket sitting across her lap.

"I'm stuck. I haven't found anything to write about. When I was with Hank it came easily because I wanted to escape, but now with Jim it's different." Grace hadn't openly admitted this to anyone, but she knew that she could at least say this to Denise. Although Grace's marriage to Hank had been terrible, Denise's relationship with him seemed to be insanely perfect. Walking through the doorway, Denise threw herself onto the loveseat with her coffee in hand, fluffing the pillows to make it a little more comfortable.

"I get it. Okay, so let me offer you a tiny distraction. Which trash panda do you want to hear about first?" Denise's mouth drew into a taunting grin. Grace's eyes widened with the prospect of something absolutely delicious. The *Trash Pandas* were a group of women in town that touted to have such perfect lives but behind closed doors they were terrible awful people with darker secrets. They would do their best to destroy good people, but truly what they were doing was making themselves feel better for the despicable lives they were living.

There were whispers of multiple affairs floating around town amongst everyone but no one confirmed whether the stories were true. Praying that Denise had all the tasty tea she could enjoy, Grace laid the unfinished blanket across her lap, straightening her posture as if Jim was standing in front of her naked, ready to be sucked off, Denise had her full and undivided attention.

"So, Roseanne Newham and Gerry Acer were caught in the B&T parking lot screwing each other in Gerry's car." Denise smiled, but Grace already had heard about this affair as a possibility. It was nice to have confirmation that someone who claimed to be so perfect in their marriage was catching something on the side, but at the same time this had whirled around for weeks.

"Boring." Grace said, now completely defeated that this was supposed to be something more interesting. Denise, however, still had a wicked grin on her lips.

"Oh no, this gets better. Rosie had a strap-on on and was giving it to him from behind when the cops showed up. They both got arrested for indecent exposure and they are calling for Gerry to step down from his job." Denise said.

Well, now that was a tasty morsel, Grace thought. It's one thing to be caught, but by a cop and to be arrested is another. The worst part of this whole scenario was the fact that Gerry worked for another township as their Code Enforcer. Part of Grace felt bad for him though.

Everyone knew Gerry's wife, Stacie, and her habitual affairs. Yet, he stayed with her despite knowing what she was doing. Every time, she would blame it on his long hours of work or the fact that he was involved in too much for the town. If that wasn't enough, she was constantly showing up to school events after hours half drunk and a few times having to be forcibly removed by the cops because she was so intoxicated.

Yet the plot twist of this whole situation that made it worse was that Rosie and Stacie were best friends. In fact, many times Grace and Nikki wondered if the two of them were having something on the side because of just how far up their asses they were. Now she figured that one or the other were just keeping their enemies close…

So, to hear that Gerry turned the tables on Stacie and slept with Rosie behind her back was something out of a great book. The wheels in her head came to a crashing halt. *Holy Shit, this would make a great book*, Grace thought to herself. She would have to change the names and situation up a little but, it would be good. It would take her a couple of months to work on it for sure, but with all the juicy gossip she had about the situation, she was sure it was salacious enough to sell.

Both Stacie and Rosie were the most vindictive one's in the Trash Panda crew and throughout the years the absolute worst to deal with. They always seemed to have their dirty little paws in everything from school or town events. Or they would make such a big uproar over things going on in the town that just being in the same room with them had become so unbearable. To make matters worse, whenever Grace and Nikki would chair any sort of event the awful trash pandas would go and undermine them. They came by their moniker "Trash Pandas" naturally.

One dance, Denise got so incensed that she went and threw out the decorations that Stacie and Rosie put up. In her defense, it wasn't out of spite. They purposely bought decorations based on the theme they had wanted but the rest of the committee voted against. When the afternoon came to set up the decorations, they had shown up early and set them all up by themselves, and when everyone showed up at the scheduled time to help, it was all done.

As Grace, Nikki and Denise trudged in the agreed-to decorations to see this, Denise saw red. Smug and proud of themselves Rosie and Stacie refused to take it all down and left. Three hours later when everyone started showing up for the actual dance, they walked into all the decorations having been tossed out in the dumpster behind the school. Denise still had a picture of them digging the decorations out of the trash and had texted them to Grace and Nikki with the only caption "Trash Pandas".

From that point on, Stacie and Rosie were forever referred to as the Trash Pandas. So, to hear about this betrayal made things so utterly delicious, and now Grace's brain started spinning.

"Okay, that is some good tea. But who is the other trash panda? Is it Stacie?" Grace was confused.

"Oh no, we have a new panda in the mix. We are now adding Brendan Moser to the list." Denise took a sip of her coffee and Grace rolled her eyes. He was an appalling human and although she wanted to know what was going on, a part of her didn't. With an arch in her brow, Grace looked over at Denise.

"He doesn't qualify as a trash panda. He qualifies as a miserable piece of shit." Grace snarked, as she reached over to put in another pod into her coffee maker. It looked like it was going to be another four cup kind of day.

"Oooohhh ho. Nooooo. I am adding him as the new trash panda. Someone walked in on him and someone having sex at the salon." Denise batted her eyes, but just the idea of Brendan having sex with someone was making Grace feel queasy. As she finished making her cup of coffee, it hit her… why would he have sex at the salon? Why wouldn't he just have sex at home? Recognizing Grace's thoughts, Denise's head bobbed up and down clearly waiting for Grace to get there.

"Hold on. It wasn't the receptionist at the salon was it? Ugh she has that terrible voice that grates on you like nails on a chalkboard." Grace asked with the same disgust you would have if you walked into a room with a week-old bag of garbage rotting away in it. Denise's mischievous laugh and quick shake of her head really had Grace's brain now totally peaked.

"Nope, better." Denise's eyes gleamed with that naughty glint that Grace loved.

"Jonathan." Denise uttered.

Doing everything possible not to spit out her coffee, Grace choked down the sip she just took and unfortunately it went down the wrong pipe. Coughing and sputtering out incoherent sounds, Grace was still trying to make sense of it. Brendan was having sex with Jonathan! Jonathan was a man. Brendan had made it his life's mission to make fun of or torment every gay male he knew. *So, since when was he into men,* Grace thought to herself.

After finally being able to catch her breath, Denise filled Grace in on what was seen and heard on both stories. However, her mind still reeled at the idea of Brendan being into other men after his past. It wasn't possible. It would mean that everything he had done and said was a complete contradiction to what they all knew.

As the smell of Grace's beef and beer stew wafted throughout the kitchen, she sat at the kitchen island writing out notes for her next book. Her concentrated silence was broken by the sound of someone trying to open the side door to the kitchen. Glancing over to the clock on the stove, she knew it was too early for Calvin or Katie to be walking in from work. As the cold wind blew through the kitchen, Kevin burst through and looked completely flushed.

"Oh my God!" Was all Kevin got out as he tried catching his breath. Grace knew exactly why he was here. He must have heard about Brendan and Jonathan. "Did you hear?" His eyes were wild and Grace wasn't sure whether she was supposed to play dumb or confess to knowing.

"What am I talking about, of course you know. But what the fuck? Why didn't you call me to tell me?" He asked, as Grace just shrugged.

"I want you to take a step back and think. Why do you care? I don't." Grace said, walking over to the pot to stir the stew silently thanking God he wasn't here to talk about the wedding.

"Um, why?" Kevin questioned. "I care because the two of them have made my life utterly miserable as of late. Of course I would want to know. So why didn't you text me?"

"Because it honestly doesn't matter." Grace said, tasting the stew to make sure it had the right balance. Kevin just huffed.

"It matters to me." Kevin retorted.

"But why? They are two miserable people. What you should be doing is focusing on other things. Things like the fact that you have the most amazing partner and fiancé. You should be focusing on your happily ever after, not these two idiots." Grace explained. Kevin's face dropped as it must have finally hit him.

"I hate you; you know that? Why do you have to be the voice of reason? Couldn't you just let me be a tiny bit petty on this?" Kevin was actually doing something he had never done before. He was conceding to Grace.

"No, it's just a waste of time. And the reason I'm the voice of reason between the two of us is because I am older, prettier and significantly smarter." Grace smiled and batted her eyes at a rather annoyed-looking Kevin. As he took in a deep breath, he pulled out a seat and peered over to see what Grace was writing.

"Older yes, prettier – I'm not hundred percent on that one." Kevin quipped, Grace looked up from her notebook narrowing her eyes on him. "Since when did you start plotting your books? You have always been a stream of conscious writer." Kevin said. Grace scrambled to close the notebook and moved it over near the stove so that she could stir the pot of stew again. She never showed anyone her books while she was writing them and even though she was sketching everything out and hadn't figured out how to change people's identities yet, she wasn't about to start sharing now.

"Well, this one needs some prepping." Grace said, not realizing that Kevin slipped quietly off his chair and snuck up behind her, stealing the notebook. Gasping at the realization of what he was doing, Grace whirled around and instantly tried to snatch the notebook out of his hand. The only problem was that he was significantly taller than she was, but she knew all the ticklish spots on him. Scrunching her fingers along his ribs she began her assault, causing his arm instantly to come down but still keeping the book at arms-length.

"Stop, give it back." Grace barked, as Kevin continued to giggle with devilish glee that he was torturing her just by having it in his hands. As the two struggled, Vivian walked into the room with a quizzical look on her face.

"Um, Grace?" Vivian said, holding her phone in her hand. Both Grace and Kevin looked up from their twisted positions and stared at her. "Uh, Katie is on the phone. She said she needs to talk to you." Grace looked at Kevin and untangled herself from his grip and realized that he would eventually read her scribbles anyway and slapped him in the arm as she walked over to Vivian.

Katie was tutoring Brendan Jr. at his mom's house so she wasn't sure why she would need to talk. Things had been going well; she just hoped that everything was alright with Kelly and the kids.

"Hey, Katie-girl what's going on?" Grace asked, placing Katie on speaker.

"Uh, well I wanted to let you know that I may be late for dinner. Kelly just got a 911 text from Mr. Moser, apparently something is going on over at the house and he called for Kelly's help. She called 911 and headed over there, but we could hear yelling in the background of the call." Katie's voice was riddled with nervousness. "It sounded like some old man was screaming at him in the background."

As Kevin and Grace locked eyes, she knew that the rumors must have hit home about Brendan and Jonathan. Mr. Moser was a staunch homophobe. If the rumors were true and his son was doing something with another man, the question on her mind was - would he actually physically harm Brendan? Kevin pulled his phone out of the back pocket of his jeans and immediately started texting and mumbling to himself. Words like, *please answer, please don't be there*, made Grace's head pop up and her mind immediately went to George. If he was working and got the call, he would have had to respond to the call and with everyone knowing that he and Kevin were together, if he was to show up, there was no telling how Mr. Moser would respond to seeing him there.

Grace's focus turned back to Katie who was still on the other side of the call.

"Listen, do you want me to come and pick you and the kids up? I have plenty of dinner here and that way they can be distracted. I'll let Kelly know they are here." Grace said, as she instantly leapt into hostess mode. Nodding to Vivian without uttering a word, Grace started heading into the TV room and started pointing to different items that needed to get picked up off the floor for Vivian to take care of. Thanking her lucky stars that they had bought this house, she went into the living room and started grabbing blankets from one of her baskets draping them over the arm of the couch.

"Yeah, it might be best." Katie said, her voice muffled as she started telling the Moser children to get their coats and shoes on and letting them know where they were going. Slipping on her shoes in the kitchen she looked over to a worried Kevin.

"Alright Katie, I'm on my way." Grace said, then turned to Kevin. "He will be fine, stay here. I'll be back in two seconds." Grabbing her jackets and keys Grace ran to her car and practically flew over to Kelly's condo.

CHAPTER SIXTEEN

George

With the temperatures dropping after the sun set, George needed to put the heat up a little higher in his cruiser. The sudden change in the weather brought a bitter cold that stung your skin and sunk right down to your bones. After comforting a young teen who had not yet learned the art of driving on slick snowy roads and speaking with the owner of the vehicle that he crashed into, George was thankful for the heated seats.

Sitting there typing out his report, praying for a quiet night, George's peaceful silence was broken by the sound of dispatch.

"Unit 22, be advised, 10-16 in progress at 423 Basher Avenue. Caller reports verbal and physical altercation between parties, possible injuries. No weapons reported. Use caution and advise when on scene. EMS on standby." The female dispatcher, Roma Kilkenny called. *So much for my quiet night*, George thought to himself. He then paused before responding. He knew that address – it was the Moser's home.

"Copy. Unit 22 enroute." George responded. Every fiber of him knew he was doing the right thing despite not wanting to get involved. Yet, he took an oath to serve and protect, and that meant even assholes like the Mosers. Mrs. Moser was a mouse of a woman, so he knew that unless she had totally snapped, it wasn't her that was the issue. But the Moser men were a different story. They were both giant humans and if they were the ones going at it then George was probably going to need back-up.

Turning the corner onto Basher Avenue, George spotted Tony Masuci just pulling up in front of the house. Scanning the area, George saw two large figures wrestling to the ground while two women stood at the front door. With only the light of the porch and streetlights, George knew the smaller woman was Mrs. Moser; however, the other woman was difficult to figure out. Parking his cruiser in front of the driveway, he took stock of the entire situation. As he surveyed it from the car, he could easily see that Brendan was bloody and decided to not even hesitate to call for EMS to respond before stepping out of the vehicle.

"Mr. Moser, please step away from your son." George called out as he approached. There was no need to ask for ID or for anyone to identify themselves. It was the small grace of living in a tiny town.

Everyone knew each other. The elder Moser's crimson face lifted from his view of his bloodied son. His eyes were seething with utter and complete contempt for anyone engaging in a conversation with him.

"This is between me and this disgusting piece of trash." His mouth foaming with spit as his words slurred together. With every tiny step Tony and George made, it was clear that Mr. Moser was not just enraged but also drunk. "Now get the fuck off my lawn and let me fix him. All he needs is another good beating."

Another? George wasn't sure what he was alluding to, but if Brendan was constantly being beaten by his father, both he and his mother needed to escape this monster. Brian Moser was well known for his temper and getting away with it. Not many people in the community liked him, but they pitied Ilene Moser.

Holding their positions, Tony and George were exactly six feet from the two males. Brendan's face was bruised and swollen as he coughed up blood, probably due to a possible punctured lung. Tony took one half step forward.

"Mr. Moser, I will repeat what the Detective said, step away from Brendan. We do not want to use any force." Tony's tone was steady and firm but still remaining as calm as possible. The very last thing that either of them wanted was to have to tase an elderly man, no matter what the situation was.

"This is my property. I can do what I want." Mr. Moser's voice grew louder. Porch lights from neighbors went on and slowly doors were opening as the scene was getting worse. George steadied his breath - he needed to remain as calm as humanly possible despite every bone in his body wanting to lunge forward and wrestle him to the ground. He looked over at Tony, who now had his hand on his taser.

"Mr. Moser, this is now a lawful order. Step away from Brendan, or I will tase you." Tony now yelled. George never once in his entire career heard him be so forceful before, but considering how this whole event was happening, for the first time he was thankful Tony was taking the lead on this. Considering Mr. Moser's bigotry, George was positive that if he were to attack anyone else it would be him.

Brian Moser stared down into his son's swollen eyes with disdain, his breathing laboring as he grabbed the collar of Brendan's shirt, pulling him up off the ground.

"You have been nothing but a disappointment your whole life." Brian spat, and Ilene took a step forward. Her cries and pleadings falling on deaf ears as she begged her husband to leave her son alone. Inching closer, George hoped that the older man would not notice as Brendan's blood-filled coughs muffled the sound of their footsteps.

"Mr. Moser, I will not say it again, this is your final warning. Step away from Brendan NOW." Tony yelled again, mere feet from him. George was now in a position that if he needed to tackle Mr. Moser he could.

"He is my son! I will deal with him the way I need to." Brian foamed as he balled up his free fist behind him ready to throw another punch. George wasn't going to let that happen. Giving a quick nod to Tony, George ran up from behind the older balding man and instantly slapped his cuffs on the hand that Brian had been ready to strike with. Instantly realizing what was going on, Brian lost his grip on Brendan's shirt and Tony was by his side assisting in restraining the seventy-three-year-old man from doing any more harm to his son.

EMS sirens wailed up the street while the two women ran to Brendan's side. Struggling to now stand, Tony took Brian into custody as George put his gloves on. Crouching down to check on Brendan, he saw relief in his eyes.

"Hang on there buddy, try not to move." George bent down. Brendan reached up and took hold of his hand, squeezing it with whatever strength he had left.

"I'm sorry." He whispered, pain etched deep in his bruised face. George's heart broke just then. "Tell Kevin, I'm so sorry." Brendan wheezed out a bloody cough as his words dripped with true regret, and as his breathing got shallower George's heart broke.

The sounds of pounding footsteps headed his way, and he turned to find Ethan and Phin of the volunteer EMS squad rushing over, ready to attend to Brendan. Rising, he watched as Tony and his Sergeant S. Heredia put Brian in the back of Tony's cruiser. Taking in a deep breath, he needed to finish the job, and he turned to Mrs. Moser and the woman standing next to her. This was the part of the calls when it came to domestic violence that he hated, the aftermath. Reaching in his top pocket, he took out his notepad and pen and braced for the story.

Turning into the parking lot of the station, George saw Kevin standing by his car. Never one to bother George during working hours, he was puzzled as to why Kevin was even here. Pulling into a spot, George reached for his phone and saw a dozen texts and missed calls. Panic hit him. What happened that he could have missed? Grabbing his gear, George haphazardly got out of the car to a worried Kevin who instantly threw his arms around him.

"I was worried sick about you. You didn't answer a single text. I heard about Brendan. Are you hurt, are you okay?" Kevin questioned, inspecting George's arms and something hit him square in the chest and he suddenly felt his nose tingling. Someone was worried about him. His love was scared about his well-being and George realized he never had this before. Never before besides his parents did a partner ever worry about him in the line of duty. As his gaze swept over Kevin, he felt the sting of tears in his eyes. He would be missed.

Locking eyes with Kevin's quizzical gaze, all George could do was grasp his face and kiss him.

"I'm fine. Brendan is at the hospital, his Dad is in custody, but I am fine." George whispered, leaning his forehead against Kevin's. Tears fell from his eyes as Kevin's whole composure melted.

"I can't lose you. I just got you and I cannot lose you now." Kevin's words caught in his throat. George's heart ached, and yet the warmth he felt in his chest spread throughout his whole body. He knew what he needed to do. He could never do this again to Kevin, the one person who had loved him from afar, worried about him even though he wasn't his. He never wanted him to panic like this ever again.

"You aren't going to lose me. I promise you." George said. "Now I have to go do something awful and terrifying right now." Kevin's eyes met his, with a hint of fear in them. "Paperwork." George joked with a sly smile.

Pulling his arms from around George's neck, Kevin slapped on the arm.

"Did you just assault an officer while on duty? I could arrest you for that." George arched his eyebrow to Kevin's defiant gaze.

"Alright you two, enough. Nicols, I need that report, pronto." Sergeant Heredia yelled from the front door of the precinct. Exchanging warm glances with Kevin, George quickly kissed him and sighed.

"Duty calls. Go home, I'll wake you when I get in." George called out as he walked into headquarters. After this specific moment he knew he had two jobs he needed to get done. His reports. And one last thing.

CHAPTER SEVENTEEN

Kevin

He hated the smell of hospitals. The medicinal odor hung in the air, with old people looking sickly or the rushing of nurses and codes being called. Kevin had gone a very long time without having to go anywhere near one since Ken suffered his heart attack. However, within the last two years it seemed that his friends and family had purchased some kind of revolving door to this place and all he wanted was to seal it shut.

But this wasn't about family. It wasn't about friends. It was about forgiveness.

Why is it always an old lady at reception, Kevin wondered. He mused that it was the idea that they would be close to medical professionals that could save their life should they have a heart attack while greeting people.

"Hello dear. Who are we here to visit?" Her name tag read Gladys. *Of course it's Gladys.*

"Brendan Moser." Kevin said. He still wasn't sure why he was even there. He really had nothing he wanted to say to him, but after George recounted what happened and what he said, Janie put her two cents in and guilt tripped him into going.

As the elderly woman handed him a guest badge he checked the room number and headed up. Kevin could just tell his parents and George that he went and made peace, but since he put that tracker link on their phones, he wouldn't be able to lie. Making his way to the room, his heart began to race. *What do you say to the person who tortured you for years? Congratulations, you got what you deserved? Get better, dickwad? Glad your dad didn't injure your asshole so you can have sex with my ex?* Kevin was sure none of those were going to be what Brendan would want to hear.

Stepping off the elevator and making his way through the maze that was the hospital, he got to his room and stopped short. He could stand here in the hallway and no one would know that he didn't talk to him.

"I can smell your cologne from here, Kevin." Brendan wheezed out from his hospital bed. *Fuck!* Taking in a deep cleansing breath, Kevin walked into the room. Brendan looked awful. Bruises and stitched up cuts littered his face. One eye was completely covered with a bandage and he looked like he had been hit by a Mack truck.

"So, you're not dead?" Kevin asked. He was at a complete loss on how to even have this conversation.

"I am not. Lucky me." Brendan smirked. The uncomfortable unease between them seemed to make the air thick and Kevin was finding it slightly harder to breathe.

"Well, you look like shit." Kevin rolled his eyes and crossed his arms.

"I feel like shit, so that tracks." Brendan's attitude had definitely changed. No longer was he the man or boy who bullied him. He'd been humbled it seemed, but Kevin was not moving any closer than just standing at the foot of his hospital bed.

"Listen, I know you don't want to be here. But I needed to say something to you." Brendan must have been feeling the tension and Kevin's resistance. "I'm sorry."

Rolling his eyes, Kevin just huffed.

"I get it, too little too late. But that is the truth. I am so sorry for how I have been."

"MY whole life! Say, I'm sorry I have been a complete and utter dick your whole life. And maybe I will consider it." Kevin snipped. This was years of pent-up anger and resentment. Years of abuse, and now his abuser was right there in front of him asking for forgiveness. But he needed to own up to it all.

"Yes, for your whole life. For how I treated you when we were younger and how I have been since I have been back." Brendan's words a tiny plea.

"Why now? Because your dad beat you, for being gay, or bi, or whatever the Hell you are? Did you think you'd get to be forgiven now?" Kevin questioned. He watched as Brendan's face softened. This was a side of Brendan he had never seen before. Brendan always looked at him with utter contempt in the past so it was odd to see such a difference. This time, the roles were reversed. For the first time in his life Kevin truly could show him without having to keep a guard up.

"No. I know that asking forgiveness is a luxury, but if you will let me explain, maybe you will understand." Brendan said. There was part of Kevin that wanted to walk away and not give his attention to Brendan any further, but if there was anything that Ken had taught him, it was that both sides of an argument needed to be heard. Resigning himself to have to endure time with Brendan, he was at least going to sit. Hesitantly grabbing the chair next to the hospital bed, Kevin placed himself down and prepared to listen.

"I had an uncle, my dad's brother Tim. It's a long story and I'm sure you don't care about my family's drama, but the gist of the story is that my Uncle Tim was gay. Basically, what it boils down to is that when I was really young, he came out of the closet and my granddad disowned him. He forced the whole family to cut ties and my dad backed him up on it." Brendan stopped for a brief moment to catch his breath. George had mentioned that he thought he had some kind of internal injuries due to him coughing up blood at the scene. He remembered how Grace was after Liz had hit her with the car and she had a punctured lung. It would take her forever just to get a whole sentence out without getting winded. "When I was really young I liked playing with my mom's dresses, they were pretty and I liked the material. I don't know why women's clothes seemed to be made of a softer fabric or something, but I liked how it felt, and to be honest, I still do. Not that you needed to know that, but I figured while I'm here might as well lay everything out on the table." Brendan smirked with a tight smile and tried steading his breath again.

Kevin just sat there in complete shock. He hadn't expected him to be so open and honest, especially about the clothes. He felt himself soften, no longer holding himself in such a stiff position. His shoulders dropped and he sat back to actually listen.

"I'm assuming you got caught?" Kevin questioned. With a slight nod Brendan let out a sigh.

"Yeah. It was when the beatings started." Brendan confirmed. All Kevin could do was shake his head.

"How old were you?" Kevin probably shouldn't have asked but he couldn't seem to help himself.

"Ten."

Kevin wasn't shocked, he was devastated. A ten-year-old merely exploring textures and styles of clothing and he was suffering beatings because of it. Kevin remembered being six years old and playing with his mother's make-up and getting caught. But instead of being beaten, his mom just smiled and helped him with the lipstick. His parents had shown him love and acceptance, not handing out beatings just for trying something against the ridiculous standards and societal norms.

"Was it just your dad or your mom as well?" Kevin asked, although he was sure it was only Mr. Moser. Mrs. Moser didn't seem like the type to even attempt to kill a fly, let alone raise a hand against someone.

"Just my dad. Mom tried to stop him once but got in the way and he hit her. She had a bruise on her face for a few days. She told people that she fell." Brendan admitted. "From that point on, if I was caught watching anything that a girl would watch, I was beaten. Being gay or interested in anything other than what a typical boy was supposed to be into, I was beaten. He shoved me into every sport known to man. When I started playing football, I actually enjoyed it. But it was the constant drumming into my head that being gay was a disease that stuck with me. If I thought like him or acted like him, then I was safe." Brendan paused to take a quick breath. "I was wrong."

"This doesn't excuse what you did." Kevin sighed.

"No, it doesn't. But when it is drilled into your brain and beaten over and over, you start to believe it." Brendan agreed as he took a small sip of water.

"It's still wrong. You could have asked for help. Any number of people in town would have helped you and your mom." Kevin said. There were so many people that he personally knew would have been there for his mother and himself.

"My mom is not the type to ask for help and I was just a kid. What was I supposed to do? Go into school and say, hey I like wearing women's clothing, and I like boys and girls but my dad is beating me because of it? Do you know how strange that sounds?" Brendan asked, as he shook his head. To him it must have made no sense, but to Kevin it made complete sense.

"YES! You were getting beaten by your dad just because you were exploring what it was to be yourself. That is enough." Kevin shrieked. He just couldn't stop shaking his head. His whole body was practically shaking with rage at the fact that this had been happening. Yet, at the same time he wasn't surprised. So many boys and girls are taught that it isn't right to like someone of the same sex or both sexes.

And if Brendan's family had a history of homophobia, it wasn't all that surprising. But to strike a child just for being different was completely insane.

"Kevin, I was getting brainwashed and beaten. He convinced me that my entire existence was messed up. That anyone who wasn't straight was a sexual deviant. I was tired of the beatings, so I chose to suppress who I really was and be what he wanted me to be to save myself." Brendan's heart rate monitor beeped; his blood pressure was up. Kevin may not have liked the guy, but he didn't need to be the cause of him having a heart attack after the beating he received.

"Okay," Kevin lowered his voice. "So why attack me? You were being persecuted at home, why target me?" This had always been the one question he could never understand.

"I was jealous." Brendan whispered. Kevin couldn't fathom what the Hell he had to be jealous of. He was the very awkward kid with a sister who got a ton of attention because of her talents.

"Of what?"

"You were loved and accepted for who you were. You were unapologetically yourself. Do you know how rare that is? To be able to just be who you are and have the support of your whole family?" Brendan asked, pain staining his words as the one bruised eye glazed with tears. Kevin's heart sank into his stomach. He was given the world, while Brendan's was taken away from him. "I was jealous. You had everything and all I saw was a kid that got to live his truth. I was angry." Brendan's voice caught and choked on a sob. "I couldn't be me, but you could. It wasn't fair."

Kevin didn't know what to say. A part of him wanted to say he was sorry. Not for any part of what happened, but for the pity he was feeling this exact moment. The whole situation wasn't right. Brendan should have been allowed to live whatever life he wanted. To be embraced, loved and cared for, but instead he was tortured and told not to be himself. A mix of anger and sadness began to overwhelm him. And then it hit him, the forgiveness. He could forgive; Brendan had been denied kindness and acceptance for long enough.

"I accept." Kevin whispered.

Brendan wiped the tears from his swollen cheek and stared at Kevin.

"No one should have gone through what you did. And although your behavior was reprehensible, I forgive you. But it comes with a condition." Kevin stood up and walked to the foot of the bed.

"Anything." Brendan replied.

"You live your life the way you always wanted to. No regrets, no fears of retaliation, you live it like you always wanted. You want to wear women's clothing, you do it. You want to date men and women, you do it. But you never intimidate, insult or hurt another living soul for living THEIR truth ever again. And, if you need help, you ask for it. Those are my terms of forgiveness." Kevin was not playing around. If Brendan was going to truly mean he was sorry then he needed to be true to himself and forgive himself as well. For a life not lived and for the path he chose.

"I can try." Brendan replied.

"There is no try. Do it. And then I will forgive you." Kevin knew the enormous step he was asking him to take, but Brendan needed to do it. Maybe not for himself, but at least for his kids. He needed to show them to accept themselves no matter what path they had to take. Kevin may not have kids of his own, but his family did and Kevin would be the first in line to show up and support them.

With a tight nod, Brendan agreed. Patting the foot of the hospital bed, Kevin bowed his head and headed out the door. The world felt different. He felt different. It was as if he had been holding something deep in his chest for years that was finally free. It wasn't hollow, it was just making room. As he got into the elevator, he took a deep breath and pressed the button for the exit. Although Brendan will have a long road to recovery, so did Kevin. Holding onto this resentment and fear for so long, he wasn't sure just what to do with himself.

He had taken that single moment all those years ago when Brendan attacked him to shape who he was as a person. To be strong, to be free and unapologetic about his sexuality. That constant state of wanting to prove someone wrong or defy their point of view drove him. And now – there was nothing. No one to fight against and the feeling unnerved him. There would always be someone, but this had been his nemesis for years and now there would be forgiveness.

"Well, I am very proud of you." Janie said with a smile, as Kevin rolled his eyes. *Of course she is, I did what she told me to do,* he thought to himself. Ken looked over the top of his newspaper and exchanged a snarky glance with his son. "So how is he doing?" Janie asked as she pulled the lasagna she had made out of the oven.

"Well, he isn't dead." Kevin responded, ripping off the end of an Italian loaf and dipping it into the pot of tomato sauce on the stove next to the resting lasagna. Janie scoffed and all Ken could do was snicker.

"Kevin Michael Cartino! That is not nice, that is not how I raised you." Janie smacked the back of his head. "He's your son, you know that. That is the kind of crap you would pull." Janie remarked looking directly at Ken. His dad's eyes grew wide in shock.

"Why am I getting dragged into this. I'm just sitting here reading." Ken asked, taking a sip of his fourth cup of coffee. Narrowing her eyes on Ken and then back to Kevin, he could feel her judging them for not caring.

"Ugh, the lot of you." Janie said, grabbing her phone and leaving the room. Kevin walked over to his father and kissed the top of his head as he continued reading.

"Alright, I'm outta here. I gotta go make dinner." Kevin reached into his coat grabbing his keys when Ken cleared his throat. Side-eyeing his dad, Kevin stopped dead in his tracks. "Um, does the peanut gallery have something to say?" Not looking up from his newspaper, Ken sighed.

"You could've at least found out how he was." Ken kept his eyes on the paper. Kevin couldn't believe that he was actually siding with his mother. He hadn't even wanted to go, why should he care about how Brendan was physically doing?

"He isn't dead. His eye is all bandaged up, he has oxygen, his color was fine minus the ghastly bruises, those looked terrible. But he's alive." Kevin retorted, annoyance oozing from his lips. Ken just shook his head.

"That's not what I mean." Ken folded his paper up and looked at his son. "His father beat him for being with a man. You just told us that he did it when he was a kid and his mother stood by completely complacent with this treatment. How do you think this makes him feel mentally? Physically it's obvious. But this wasn't just physical abuse, this was a level of mental abuse no one should suffer." Kevin's stomach was turning into knots. "You are fortunate, you know that right? You have parents, family and friends that accepted you. Now I want you to imagine if that hadn't been the case and add beatings to the mix. Deep inside I need you to realize that this was a broken man, raised by broken people. Was what he did to you wrong? Yes, but he wasn't taught any better. Should you forgive him? You know your mother is going to say that it will get you into heaven, but I'm not gonna catholic guilt you. All I am going to say is that life is too short to carry around the weight of old grudges and that hopefully he will get the mental help he needs and you two can find a path of peace."

Damn it! Kevin hated when his dad got all wise and made sense.

"I don't want to be his friend." Kevin stated. Ken nodded.

"Fair, boundaries are good. Listen, I'm not saying become his best friend, just be the good neighbor and person I know you are and if he reaches out to talk, just be there to listen." Ken wasn't exactly asking. It was more of him telling him to do the right thing. To be the man, he knew Kevin was.

As he stood on the front door of the Mosers' porch with a basket of homemade goodies Kevin knew what he was doing was the right thing. He didn't want to, but he was doing the right thing. A week after Brendan was released from the hospital, Kevin received a text asking him for help. George had told him he didn't need to go if he didn't want to but his father's words hung too heavy in his heart. Ringing the doorbell, the door opened not a second after and there stood Brendan, shocking Kevin at how quickly he answered.

"Uh, hi." Kevin uttered. In the light of day, he could see just how badly Brendan had suffered. His face actually looked worse now that the bruises were starting to fade into that grossly weird yellowish green with hints of purple around them.

"Hi, thank you for coming by. I didn't know who to ask about something." Brendan stuttered, he was nervous. The once tall and confident man had transformed into something different. The overweight beaten man in front of him was very timid and calm and the whole thing was making Kevin feel weird. "Please come in."

The smell of mothballs hung in the front hallway and he gathered it was probably coming from what he was guessing was a coat closet. Mrs. Moser walked through the hall and smiled brightly to Kevin.

"Oh, Kevin, it is lovely to see you. I told Brendan that I am happy to help, but he thought perhaps you would be able to help him out a little better than his old mother could." Ilene's voice was warm and filled with joy for some reason.

"I am not even sure why I'm here. All you said was that you needed help, so I'm here." Kevin passed the gift basket over to the tiny woman whose smile went even bigger as he just looked around. Their home was dated but decorated in a very minimalistic approach. It was clean but oddly there was a tray table by the recliner that sat alongside it with make-up on it.

"I didn't know who would help me without judging me, and you said if I needed help you would." Brendan slowly made his way to the recliner and cautiously sat down in it. "Kelly is bringing the kids by and the last time they came they didn't come near me because of what my face looks like. I was hoping you could teach me how to put make-up on so the kids won't be afraid."

Kevin's heart broke instantly, but something from his youth echoed in his head, *"be the good, be one of the helpers"*. Walking towards him, Kevin perused the assortments of foundations and cover-ups that were there. It wasn't great, but it would at least make it a little easier for the kids and for Brendan.

"A part of me wants to be slightly offended because this skin," pointing to his own face "doesn't have a stitch of make-up, just a tinted moisturizer. But if I remember correctly, your make-up the day you attacked me was atrocious. If you did that yourself, brother, you did an awful job." Kevin said as he examined Brendan's face. A tiny gasp came from behind and he realized Mrs. Moser had come back into the room.

"I did his make-up that time." Ilene's voice tinged with a hint of sadness. Kevin suddenly felt bad and needed to recover from offending her.

"Oh sweetie, I'm sorry. Listen, men's faces have different bone structures. I'll help him out. You can learn in case you need to do this again." Kevin offered, but Brendan shook his head.

"No, teach me. Just something simple." Brendan's voice determined and the one eye that wasn't still covered with an eye patch seemed to gleam. Kevin smiled, nodding in approval.

"Alright sir, let's figure out your base." Kevin said as he started searching through all the products on the table.

EPILOGUE

George & Kevin

George

December 29, 2025

As George stood in the hallway of the precinct, a part of him felt like it did the first day on the force. His heart was fluttering so fast that he actually felt sick. A voice rang out through the speakers in the hallway.

"Toselle Park police, dispatch and volunteers please stay tuned for a special announcement." Three tones rang out through the speakers and George could feel the sweat starting as his heart raced. "It is with great pleasure to announce that as of 15:00 hours on December 29th, 2025, after over 20 years of service that Detective George Darius Nicols, member 1143 of the Toselle Park Police Department, will be retiring from service. The members of the Toselle Park Police Department would like to congratulate you on your retirement. We want to extend a heartfelt thank you for serving the residents of Toselle Park with great pride, integrity and true professionalism. You will be sorely missed and want to wish you all the best in your next chapter of your life. It has been an honor and privilege to serve with you."

George was having a tough time trying to see through the tears in order to grab his mic. Blinking them away, he brought his mic to his face. "TP R1143 to County."

"County answering."

"After 20 plus years of serving as a Toselle Park Police Officer it has been my pleasure and honor to serve our town. Today is my final day of service. I am not one for flowery words but it has been my pleasure to be a member of such an amazing police force and community. Thank you all for making my job so easy. I want to thank my parents, family and my wonderful husband-to-be Kevin for always having my back. Thank you. TP R1143 I will be 10-8."

"On behalf of County dispatch, we would like to wish you all the best and many happy years in your new adventure. As of 15:00 hours you are officially 10-8."

George looked down the empty hallway and took one final breath in. He was retired. Turning, he looked out the door to the entirety of the staff, fire department, EMS, friends and family standing outside. As he walked out the doors, bagpipes immediately started playing as the color guard and staff were called to attention.

Breathing was hard.

He had spent so much of his life just working, and now he would have the time in the world. The panic that coursed through him the week leading up to this day had actually caused him to have a few panic attacks. However, Kevin seemed to be an old pro on getting through them and helped every breath of the way.

As he stared down the long line of fellow officers, his brother and sisters in arms, his lip started to quiver and his eyes seemed to have a tough time coming into focus. Taking in another deep breath, it was time to start living his life.

A salute was called and as he saluted his co-workers, he held his head high because at the end of the long line of people stood his future. Kevin stood there with tears in his eyes and love in his heart and it all belonged to him.

Kevin

December 31, 2025

"It is fucking snowing, whose stupid idea was it that you guys get married on New Years Eve?" Kevin asked as he brushed the snow out of his hair while he followed Hank into the hotel lobby. The little sneaky devil, that Denise was quietly put the whole thing together in just a matter of weeks without anyone's help. Grace and Nikki spent two weeks yelling at her right before George's retirement about how they were supposed to help her with all the planning, but it fell on deaf ears.

"She wanted to go to Vegas. Nikki would have killed me if I let her." Hank added as he brushed the snow off his overcoat and took it off. His black tuxedo looked really good on him if you asked Kevin, but then he spied someone else wearing a better one.

George was pinning a boutonniere to Philippe's lapel and it was taking everything within Kevin not to tackle him to the ground and having his way with him. There was a tiny part of him that also was slightly pissed at Denise. After she had sprung this whole thing up on them, Kevin had begged her to make it a double wedding considering that he and George had plans to go on a cruise the following month. It would have been a perfect honeymoon, but Denise wouldn't have it. He remembered just how pissed she got at him when he mentioned the idea a few weeks earlier at yoga.

"Get your own damn wedding! I worked hard putting this together." Denise argued. Kevin knew he was being too indecisive as to when to have the wedding. Earlier in the week George looked at him and suggested the following September, but a tiny part of him was secretly thinking about having it on Halloween.

"Grace doesn't seem to want to help me. Why can't we just make it a joint wedding?" Kevin pressed. Denise whirled around mid-tree pose and pushed him.

"Because I've never been married and I want my own. If you weren't so damned wishy-washy about when you want it then maybe Grace would help. So go figure your own shit out. You can't steal my wedding." Denise went back to her mat and took a deep breath in trying to center herself and went back to her yoga routine. She was right. They needed to pull the trigger and pick a date. But first to get George through his retirement ceremony.

"Philippe, she's upstairs in room 414. She texted me that you can go up there. I apparently am supposed to be waiting in the solarium with you two with bated breath." Hank said, flashing both Kevin and George the text. Kevin snickered to himself; Denise had been so calm and collected up until this past week. Jodi had been practicing a piano piece for the first dance at all hours of the night; Phillippe was insisting on paying for the honeymoon if she wasn't going to allow him to pay for the wedding and Hank had just gotten a cold. Several times Denise had come banging on his door in the middle of the day to just vent to Kevin about it. The day after Christmas she came over just to take a nap, claiming that she just needed a fifteen-minute power nap. Three hours later, George woke her up to let her know that dinner was ready if she wanted something to eat. As Kevin watched a bleary-eyed Denise stumble out of his room and then look pathetically to George, he knew how blessed he was to have him. George held her swaying there as she finally let all of her frustration go. He fell a little bit more in love with him right that moment.

As Kevin took the boutonniere for Hank out of the package he heard the ding of the elevator. There, walking out in the stunning mermaid silhouette gown and flowers in hand was Denise, Grace and Nikki. Whirling Hank around so he wouldn't see, Kevin looked at the three women and just shook his head.

"She is right behind me isn't she?" Hank asked. Kevin blinked up to him but didn't answer. The clacking of Denise's heels echoed through the reception area and Kevin's eyes widened as she marched right up to the back of Hank.

"Didn't I text you to be waiting at the altar with bated breath?" She questioned. Fear spread across Kevin's face, but all Hank could do was smirk.

"So now you are the one giving orders?" Hank said, looking at Kevin, but he knew he wasn't talking to him.

"I thought good boys listen and do as their told?" Denise whispered, now standing pressed against the back of Hank. Kevin could only watch as Hank's pupils dilated right in front of him as he struggled to pin the boutonniere onto his coat.

"And I thought, I gave the orders, not take them?" Hank snarked back. He was actively flirting with Denise right in front of Kevin.

"Ew, gross. I'm done. I'll see you two inside." Kevin shook his head in disgust. But he understood them, it was years of the two of them fighting to somehow turn into a romance. But now they were finally with the right person. As he walked over to George his disgust melted away. He had his person and he couldn't be happier.

George

October 31, 2026

As the sun set over the mountains, the leaves that were already turning to the burnt orange that Kevin loved so much seemed to shine like tiny gems of amber breezing in the wind. After finally getting Kevin to pick a date, George was just happy it was finally all going to be over. As he turned around to the crowd of friends and families that surrounded him he caught sight of the most perfect husband walking down the aisle. Kevin opted for an all-black tuxedo as his parents walked him down the aisle.

George's breath caught in his throat as he watched a nervous Kevin getting closer, tiny streams of tears glistening on his cheeks. George spent the week before needing to calm him down a few times as Kevin went into full Bridezilla mode, but this all made up for it. His heart raced as he was about to make his best friend his whole world.

After retiring from the force, he and Kevin made sure to take time to do some things around the cabin to make it fit their needs. They turned one of the bedrooms into a gym and Kevin selected the perfect corner in the living room to set up his office space. But that was just the cabin. The two had finally decided to go on a vacation, which only made George completely uncomfortable as he was used to a more regimented day. Going on vacation meant you could do whatever you wanted, whenever you wanted. On the first day of their cruise they took in January he remembered how lost he felt.

He wasn't sure why he was up, showered and already dressed sipping on his cup of coffee on their private balcony at six a.m. but here he was. George thought that he would get used to sleeping in, but his body still woke up early. As the cool sea breeze blew across his face, he was thankful that they had warmer weather in the Caribbean than up at home in NJ. He stared off into the horizon wondering what new and exciting things he and Kevin could do with the rest of their lives, but nothing came to mind. They could finally pick a date. It would have to be something meaningful. The place would need to be somewhere that meant something to the two of them.

The Sun Porch was where they first kissed, but he highly doubted Kevin would want to have his reception there. He knew Kevin loved Christmas Eve, but Kevin was impatient, so it would need to be sooner. As his eyes scanned the ocean, it hit him. Getting up from his seat, he walked back into their cabin and walked over to Kevin still sleeping in bed.

Bending down, kissing Kevin's bare shoulder, he enjoyed the hum from Kevin as the skin under his lips prickling from that tiny gesture. Smiling to himself, George did it again, to try and wake Kevin up, fortunately he succeeded. As Kevin rolled over, a sleepy smile spread across his lips as he blinked up to George.

"It's too early! Why are you awake?" Kevin pouted.

"Halloween at the cabin." George said, leaving Kevin to rub his eyes, shaking his head trying to follow what he was saying.

"I'm sorry, you are awake because Halloween at our cabin? Grace hosts Halloween." Kevin sounded completely lost as he slow blinked up to George, who now was very excited about the prospect he had just thought up.

"We get married on Halloween at our cabin. Halloween is very important to both of us, and the cabin is the first place I told you that I loved you. So, there is no other place that I want to solemnly swear that I will love you forever. In our home, on our special day." George explained. Kevin's eye glazed over with tears as he reached up throwing his arms around George's neck bringing him in for a kiss.

"I love you. I don't know what I would do without you." Kevin confessed. But the truth was George didn't know what he would do without him.

But now with his person standing in front of him before all that loved them, his whole life felt complete. No longer was he searching for someone, because that one had been there the whole time. As he took Kevin's hands in his, he looked up in his chocolate brown eyes and whispered. "Hi."

Kevin smiled. George had finally told him all about his dream and from that moment on anytime he said that simple word, Kevin would tear up.

"Hi." Kevin whispered back. A tiny noise of someone clearing their throat made them both turn to the noise. Nikki looked up at the two of them.

"I need to start this before you two idiots start professing your vows without my cue. I didn't get ordained for no reason." Nikki scolded the two huge men that stood in front of her. The group of loved ones surrounding them all chuckled. It was the reason they had chosen Nikki to do the ceremony. Grace would have cried, Denise would have been too blunt, but Nikki would have made it a great mix of sweetness with a dash of humor.

Nikki smiled, "My ghouls and goblins, living and dead. We are gathered here on this mountain to join together these two beautiful souls in the sanctity of matrimony." Somewhere after that George couldn't seem to hear a single thing, all he did was stare into the eyes of Kevin and thought, *my best friend, my love, My Person.*

The End.

ABOUT THE AUTHOR

G.M. Parrillo is the quintessential Generation X "Jersey Girl." Growing up in the Garden State, it is only natural that G.M. is happiest with dirt under her nails as she digs in her garden with her two boys and dachshund, Pennie, right by her side, or with her toes buried in the sand as she sits on the beach with her husband at the Jersey Shore.

As a child, struggling with a learning disability, her mother encouraged her to become a bookworm and, in doing so, she found herself inspired to write her own stories, but only for her own personal enjoyment, until now.

My Person is for all those who have been ostracized for their choice of who they love and who they are. This is G.M. Parrillo's debut completed series - The Toselle Park Series. She is currently collaborating with Amanda Kilkenny on a children's book series called The Curious Crew Chronicles and is working on her next top-secret project. G.M. is also a founding member of The Inkbound Society and Bookshop located in Gort, County Galway, Ireland. You can find her on her listed social media pages on her website – www.gmparrillo.net.

The Toselle Park Series:
A Fall for Grace
Bad Decisions
My Person